VOICES FROM HELL

Jason Park

DEDICATION

To my mom and dad

I wrote this novel as a gift, but also as an explanation of what you have made possible for me. The story of a college teenager as a replica of how the power of belief can create opportunities, like you the belief guys have had in me.

Table of Contents

PROLOGUE

Sound – vibrations that travel through the air and can be heard when they reach a person's or animal's ear. For years, I took this sense for granted, as well as all my opportunities to succeed in different ways, but everything changed.

Throughout my intense but relatively short forty seven years of life, I have heard just about every sound in existence, but truly none as strange as the one I kept hearing on the night of October 12, 1996. That night, I was out with my friends, enjoying a typical Saturday night, leaving the stress of my college life at Harvard behind, along with most of the other thoughts a normal engineering major would have during their sophomore year.

Of all things, the senses are something I have never seemed to grasp fully. It's not that the ability to hear or see is particularly complicated, but it still feels so different from everything else. Throughout my life, I've always been the guy to come up with new theories, which is probably the reason I even got into the school that I did.

It's weird. From the day I was born up until this echo of sound, I had never really believed in any type of magic—especially the kind that results in bad dreams after bad dreams, leaving anyone wondering if they were insane. This night and experience weren't just something that changed my perception of what was possible; instead, they brought me to a new place of trust I had only previously heard about.

At the time, I wasn't some popular kid with a ton of faith in people. In fact, I was damn near the opposite. The school wasn't as hard for me as it was for everyone else; it was just my unchanging awkwardness that prevented me from forming the kinds of trust or relationships every other kid seemed to build so quickly.

When writing this, I sometimes get confused by the unquestioned curiosity of the situation. Not necessarily about why it was me, but more about whether it even happened or if I was still dreaming that day almost 30 years ago. Life was so different back then—not just because of technological changes, but more importantly, in how people thought about life. Funny enough, I wish this had happened in today's media-centered world to see the public's reaction when something like this would almost certainly go viral.

When reading this, all I ask is an open-minded perspective. The story of a struggling teenager in college may seem simple, but when perceptions and traces of reality begin to conflict, it can become very confusing—even for me. This story isn't meant to prove anything but instead to reveal a slit of reality and how different something can be if you just listen correctly.

CHAPTER 1
A NIGHT IN OCTOBER

As I walked out of my class that day at around 3:00 p.m., I honestly didn't have any idea where to go. Usually, I would meet with the few friends I had, study for some test I was likely to fail, or sleep, thinking about my life and what could have been if I wasn't so terrified of being anyone but myself. It was a Friday, not some random weekday, but a day near the beginning of my sophomore year that gave me the long-lasting break I desperately needed after the previous four days. To this day, I never really know why I went to Harvard. I mean, I know my mom was happy, and being able to give her something back after raising me and my brother alone was the least I could do.

As grim as my life seems right now, I promise it's better than most of the people around me. The amount of stress roaming through the campus pathways this early in the year was contagious and something I never really understood until this year. Most of my friends didn't even go to Harvard, so being here was not the ideal life if my goal was to have fun. As I walked past groups of people in their dark maroon, silently whispering about their plans for the weekend, I started to think about mine. What could I do? Could I somehow make something out of the ordinary this weekend, this Friday? Looking back on it, I guess I was right, but the scared-to-breathe person I was would have run to death if he knew what would occur. I never really understood why I was so passive in my mind, whether it stemmed from my great life that I tried to feel bad about or another element—something countless psychiatrists had tried to figure out. This might seem dramatic to whoever is reading this, but that's just the type of person I was.

My few friends knew this, which is why when I went back to my shared apartment that afternoon, I was immediately texted, asking if I wanted to hang out that night at an amusement park. Like I said, most of my friends weren't from Harvard, so the idea that they didn't want to party but instead wanted to hang with me was surprising when it came to a weekend so early in the year.

I know they were my friends, but when I'd ask, I'd generally get some response about some fraternity event or group they had to meet instead of the rapid-fire "yes" I learned to expect in high school. Like I said though, that afternoon was different, and I was ready for it. As I got back to my apartment, I quickly texted back, wondering what the plan was for the night. Like I've said, I wasn't a very extroverted kid comparatively, which helped me in my studies but not in the pursuit of friends or, in my situation, a girl. As I sat at my desk, finishing up some work, I daydreamed of what could be: what it would be like to finally have a core group of friends to hang out with every weekend, whether or not I picked the right college and other random ideas that come to a kid's head when he's bored on a Friday afternoon. More than anything, my life confused me. I wondered why I wasn't as busy as my friends. Even if I was hypothetically on a better path in life because of Harvard, the excitement they had every day compared to my mindset of just getting through, seemed oddly depressing every time I stupidly decided to consider it.

The next text I got was from Amy, Will's longtime girlfriend and the one girl I trusted, which might sound awful, but it was just how my life panned out.

Amy: "Hey Jesse, meet us down by the outlet, and we can drive over to the park; plus, there's a girl I want you to meet."

I would be lying if I said these words didn't scare me. As I said, I wasn't very good at meeting people, not because I gave off a bad first impression, but instead, I honestly never could come up with the words to sway a girl one way or another. I tried to expand and get better with the help of my friends. But all that created was more awkward situations instead of the distasteful looks I previously got. As I got ready, I freaked out, much less than I would later that night looking back on it, but more than I normally did when picking what to wear. Amy had previously tried to set me up, but for some reason, tonight felt different. It felt like the night I would finally push through and find a girl who understood me for who I was as a thinker as opposed to some party-loving frat boy like my friends.

I started driving over, thinking about all the night's possibilities, mainly to take my mind off what I was most worried about. I don't even know why I thought this night would be different. It's not like October 12th was some holiday or some special family event. It just seemed like a night to turn my life around. Now, anybody who knows me would probably laugh at this as saying this is something I had done multiple times before in different scenarios. For context, there were at least five times back in high school when I told my friends that I would go and talk to my crush and make a move, and I never did, so this time, I figured I would keep this idea to myself.

As I drove, I saw the yawning sun going down on this chilly night. It's not an abnormal thing, but, like I said, something to keep my mind off of the "task at hand." I wasn't a huge fan of scenery, but it was something that intrigued my overall ideas of why things would happen. Looking back on that night almost thirty years ago, that thought would pierce my mind every night after. But at the time, it seemed like a playful thought to think about when I was in a thinking state.

As soon as I parked, Will jogged over to me, warning me about what Amy told me, almost like for the first time, they weren't on the same page when it came to setting me up.

Will: "I'm telling you, bro, she's kind of a weird chick, maybe exactly your type," he said while laughing, "but seriously, just take your time with it, and don't freak out on the rides like you did last time."

Not only did I have to meet some new girl, I had to get on roller coasters which wasn't the most calming experience.

I walked with Will down to the main building where Amy was parked and immediately saw the girl they kept discussing. To my surprise, it wasn't some random weird girl, but instead, a girl that I had known for years. In high school I was her main help in trying to pursue my friend while I tutored her.

"Kira?" I said as I saw her, much relieved that it was her but also confused as to why she would agree to hang out with me when work wasn't involved.

Kira: "Jesse! Oh my gosh, it's been so long!"

It was weird; she seemed much more excited about the opportunity than I had thought. Was she just as nervous as me to meet someone new? Was she messing with me to make me feel stupid when I never really had a chance? I decided to take the first question and run with it, hoping that even with our past, I would have a real opportunity to get to know her, and then, who knows what would happen. As we got in the car, my breathing slowed to a steady pace, mostly because I would be more comfortable talking to the girl instead of sitting there in fright, figuring out what words to say.

The first part of the ride was silent for the most part, well besides Will's constant need to sing to the songs, thinking he was some modern-day Elvis impersonator, and Amy, who, to her unknowingness, was making the situation between Kira and myself more awkward than it already was shaping to be. After trying to pass the time on my phone, I looked over at Kira, thinking of what to say. As nervous as I was, I had to find something to say, even if it provided some dismissive awkwardness.

"You like roller coasters, Kira?" I asked with a slight tension in my voice, not because I feared her reaction but more so because of my mental uncertainty about what to say in situations like these.

Kira glanced up from her phone, looking at me with the same face I remember thinking about when I still thought I had a chance with her back in high school. Kira was a unique girl in the sense that she was never inherently mean, but she also gave almost no signals in terms of what she thought of a person unless she was drunk.

Kira: "Yeah, I mean, it's pretty late, so I don't know what will be open. I'm just happy to get out of that college," she said as she smiled, showing her beautiful lip gloss.

I nodded, looking down at myself, trying to process what she had said. I was searching for the perfect response—something that would keep the conversation going instead of letting it fizzle out as quickly as it had started.

As I replayed her words in my mind, I glanced at the clock. It was already nine p.m. Somehow, the past few hours had slipped away, and I had only managed to muster a single sentence in all that time.

About twenty minutes later, we got out, parked, and walked into the park as a group, hoping that we weren't too late to experience the park for what it was. Amy and Will walked slightly ahead of Kira and me, who acted more awkward than ever, even though we had hung out multiple times prior to that with a group of our friends. Through the walk to the first ride, I managed to get out a couple of sentences to her as we discussed college life so far and the differences from the high school world we had grown so accustomed to in the past.

Every time I began to talk about college; however, it turned me into this depressed and unspoken person I never want to be. My guess was that it reminded me of the mistake I made when coming to the decision, but at least my mom was happy.

The night started to get better as we went on the first couple of rides. More excitement between all of us finally allowed my personality to begin to come out, which created better communication between everyone, including Kira and myself.

When I look back, it seems so weird how I predicted almost everything about that night without even knowing it. Not only did I think of the importance of the night and the outcome, but for the first time in my life, I had a feeling that the night would take a turn at one point that would take everything in me to surpass.

After the third ride, we sat down to eat at the one place that was still open: a little cafeteria called Minty's. I had eaten there a couple of times, and while it was nothing special, it was food which, at that point, was a pretty good compromise. As we sat there, scrolling on our phones, I felt a twitch in my arm, almost like a shock someone would get out of being nervous or insecure. I ignored it, thinking it was just a feeling of nervousness due to the anticipation I had for the night. The only person who noticed was Will, who looked at me like I had just told a joke, smirking at me while still giving me a face of a combined question and concern I knew him for.

Will: "Jesse, you all right, bro? What was that demonic ass shake thing you just did?"

I laughed back, telling him it was nothing, but his words were stuck. Why did he use the word "demonic"? Maybe I was overthinking it, but using a word I always had associated with some bible myth made me stop for a second and consider the words. Like I said prior, I wasn't super big into faith as a kid. I loved theories and everything to do with thought, but putting a known religious word into a description of something I did terrified me.

As a Harvard engineering major, people might have thought it was weird for me even to have the time to think about such thoughts, but it honestly became one of my main priorities when it came to my free time. I was just sitting by myself in a room in a dorm, thinking about what could change. Whether it was the reality of something like religion or the possibilities in our future, I always just wrote down whatever came to my mind in a journal-like way without the emotional side that most journals show.

Anyways, we got up shortly after, walking out of the dinner and to the center of the park. Due to the seasonal aspect of it and the year turning to October, the park was hosting events in the central area with games, food, and just more interactive things most parks would do for the family audience. As we walked around, I kept thinking about what Will said. Even the conversations I was having at the time seemed clouded, as for the first time in my life, I couldn't get an idea out of my head when I wanted to. As a person who loves to think, I could typically quickly shift between ideas, but not this time. It was almost like I had been overtaken by whatever caused the tension in a way where I wasn't even thinking about Kira for the first time that day.

Amy: "Okay, everyone, we should get some snacks before playing the games. I don't know if I'm ready for a roller coaster this soon after such a big meal."

We all nodded, agreeing with her, and as Kira left with Will across the field to grab some food, another feeling of sudden fright hit me. This time, it wasn't just a shudder but more of a higher-pitched yell in my brain, something any normal person like myself wouldn't think anything of due to its uniqueness. This time was different, though, maybe because it was just

Amy and me bickering, or perhaps it was because of the tension I felt earlier, but the moment made me pause. As I stood there next to Amy, I felt alone for the first time in my life. Being alone wasn't having anything to do in a college dorm. Being alone isn't going to sleep in your house every night with nobody around to check on you. No, being alone in those phases was nothing compared to this.

Amy quickly noticed something was off and shook my shoulder, which luckily took me out of the trance I was in and brought me back to some sense of a temporary reality. Internally, I was as scared as anyone, but due to the sounds and people around me, there remained some safety that pushed me through the line with her before we grabbed the snacks, meeting back up with Will and Kira.

As soon as we saw them, Amy called Will over and started to converse with him in some sort of secretive way, clearly not wanting their conversation to be heard by anyone at the park, including Kira and I. As I watched, Kira walked over to me, asking if I had any idea what they were talking about. I glanced at her, not knowing what to say, before blurting out, "I had another episode, like how Will was talking about the demonic movements, like one of those." To this day, I couldn't tell you why I told her, but I was glad I did. For the first time in my life, I had trusted someone with information that I honestly didn't know that well. Maybe it was because my mind was so clouded, but I just felt like Kira was the right person to tell, the right person not to know me enough to judge me compared to my normal personality.

Kira: "Oh ok, well I couldn't tell you why that's happening, but if you need help or something with your disease, let me know," she said, smirking, like what Will did back at dinner.

I didn't know at that time if I was wrong for trusting her or whether she was trying to hide her compassion, but either way, it didn't make me feel any better. Another word in her phrase struck me, however: I had now had 2 "episodes" and two different words used to describe such a thing: "disease" and "demonic." Like I keep saying, I've always tried not to take their words to heart, but again, I couldn't just gloss over them without any thought. I guess it felt a little different from Kira since she really didn't know me very well. Honestly, she probably thought that I had developed some type of aneurysm over the past couple of months, making me straight-up crazy.

Amy and Will walked back over, not saying anything, but seemed to be hiding some fear that I could only guess was for me. What they didn't know, however, was that their fear was nothing in comparison to mine. I truly had no inconceivable thought to what was developing. As we continued to walk around, the emptiness inside of me continued to halt any happiness I wanted to have. It wasn't nearly as prevalent as before, but the emotion I felt carving into my heart was still something I didn't know how to describe. It was almost like a combined feeling of a person close to you getting hurt but feeling guilty and joyous about it at the same time. Thinking more about said description, I think it sounds demonic the more I think about it. Saying anything joyous about an injury is something that goes against any moral I have or ever had before that night and something I have never felt since.

As we reached the next game, surrounded by roller coasters on every side, the feeling started to return. This time, it was weirder, stronger, stranger, and cloudier. I couldn't even distinguish between the terrors of the noise and the bustling sound of the roller coasters. As the noises grew louder, I glanced at Kira, who seemed preoccupied, wondering if I was insane or if it was just the coasters I had mentioned earlier. She looked at me with the same confused expression as before, her face a mix of discomfort and uncertainty. She shook her head—not confirming or denying anything—and that only deepened my fear, leaving me in a sense of trance-like dread.

As I approached the game, the sounds intensified. The balls I was throwing felt heavier, and as I stepped away, I stumbled, consumed by a true sense of fear. The sounds weren't quiet and definitely weren't coming from the roller coasters. Instead, they were crying-like sounds—not sad cries, but scared ones— accompanied by words of terror I'll never forget: *"Is this home? What is this place? How did I get here?"*

I froze, completely still for a few seconds, my hands unknowingly clasping my ears. The balls I held dropped onto the concrete below. I didn't know what to do. The voices around me sounded muffled—not because my ears were covered, but as if whatever I was hearing demanded to be the only thing in my mind. Usually, such sounds wouldn't have affected me, but the more I tried to ignore them, the louder they grew. What began as the yelp of one child evolved into what seemed like a collective cry for help—a group of young children trapped in some surreal, dreamlike scenario. The only thing that broke through my spiraling thoughts was the feel of Will's hand on my back as he softly asked if I was okay.

I turned to him in confusion, praying to God I wasn't losing my mind. But the more I looked around, the more it felt like I was. The only words I could force out were:

Jesse: "Do you guys hear that? Like, almost a scream?" I asked, shaking internally at a vicious rate, wondering if I was going crazy.

Will: "What are you talking about, Jesse? I mean, maybe from the roller coasters, but nothing out of the ordinary—or, you know, demonic," he added in an almost sarcastic tone.

That word again—*demonic*. Now, more than ever, I started to believe him. Not because I wanted to, but because I didn't know what or who to believe anymore. The more I thought about these terrors, the louder they became. The sounds grew weirder, like a deep, visceral nightmare with no tangible source.

I stumbled around the area before collapsing onto a small bench, desperately trying to think of a way to silence the relentless noise. I had no idea what to do.

The only person who didn't seem to think I was crazy was Kira, but that was only because she was too preoccupied with her cotton candy to notice anything I was saying or doing.

As I looked up at the sky; I had no idea what was happening. What were these sounds? What were they saying? Who—or what—was speaking?

These questions swirled through my mind, growing louder and more overwhelming until I felt myself slipping further into a chaotic spiral of thought. I finally collapsed, falling back off the bench and onto the dirt below in an uncontrollable faint. It was too much.

CHAPTER 2
WHAT NOW

As I woke up, I truly didn't know how to feel. I didn't know what time it was, what had happened, why I wasn't still at the park, or any of the other questions someone might ask after passing out. The only thing I could recognize around me was a couple of strands of black hair that reminded me of Kira. I tried to sit up, but the harder I tried to make my body function, the more impossible it became. Not knowing why, I panicked, screaming the way someone might if they were being brutally tortured.

Kira ran in, looking just as worried as I felt. She rushed over to me, her voice trembling as she spoke.

Kira: "Jesse, Jesse, chill out, ok? You're in a hospital and very weak. Just let your body rest."

I looked up at her in confusion, wondering why she was so calm, all while forgetting that I was the only one who seemed to be losing my mind.

"Kira?" I croaked, my voice breaking as though it were worn out from hours of shouting. "What happened last night?" I didn't even know what else to say. Even though I was weak, I felt an urge to speak—more for a sense of normalcy or comfort than anything else.

She looked at me with concern. While she answered, explaining how I had fainted, there was something in her voice that seemed off, something she was trying to hide. I started to pick up on it, using the small amount of mental clarity I still had.

Kira explained how Will and Amy had left shortly after the paramedics arrived due to curfew. She also mentioned how she had instructed the medics not to run any tests and how terrified she felt, thinking I might not make it.

Wasn't going to make it? I thought about this for a few long seconds. Never during the entire episode I'd experienced did I consider the possibility of death. I guess if I had taken Will's and Kira's descriptions to heart, I might have, but at this point, my time in this reality was the last thing on my mind.

As time passed, I started to regain my strength. A couple of hours later, I managed to sit up—primarily due to Kira's presence and her uplifting words. Getting back to normal was all I cared about at that moment.

When I finally stood up, still struggling to make sense of everything, I glanced over at her again, trying once more to figure out if she knew anything. "Hey, Kira, be honest with me—do you have any idea what happened or why?"

I think she could tell how desperate I was for any answer, any clarity she could offer.

Kira: "I don't know, Jesse. I mean, I heard faint sounds, but nothing like the terror you seemed to be overtaken by."

She said it with a hint of sarcasm, as if she still couldn't quite believe what I had gone through. Even though she had been right next to me during the whole event, she seemed unshaken by the idea that I might not be insane but rather *overtaken.*

I took a few sips of water and nodded at her, trying to mask my confusion about her answer and the lingering feeling inside me. Unlike the voices and tension I had experienced earlier, this feeling was different—more emotional. It was a mix of fear and confusion, so intertwined that I couldn't separate the two.

I got up and looked around, searching for anything to distract me from the reality of the situation. The glistening moon, a striped bag lying in the corner, a dimmed lamp hanging from the ceiling—anything that felt out of the ordinary, something that might bring a sliver of light to such a cloudy scene.

The more I looked, the more my mind raced.

Why couldn't I focus on anything but the emotions still consuming me?

Why was Kira acting so strangely about what had happened?

These questions swirled in my head, relentless and unyielding, as I sat back down. I took occasional sips of the liquid I'd been prescribed, but it did little to settle me. I felt lost in the ruins of my fragmented thoughts.

Kira glanced at me as though she was still trying to piece together what had happened—or at least, that's how it seemed to me. Suddenly, she blurted out: *"Screams. Choirs of terror. Reality or a dream."*

I sat bolt upright, staring at her in fright. Was this how other people felt around me? Was Kira just as insane as I seemed to be? I didn't know, but I had to ask.

"Kira? First off, are you okay? And second, what just happened? Was I not the only one?"

She looked down at her feet, her expression heavy with what seemed like despair, before answering in a quiet, solemn voice.

Kira: "Yes and no, Jesse. Yes, I'm fine, and I know what happened—or at least, I know what you experienced—but no, I didn't experience it with you last night. I honestly couldn't tell you what your situation was at the park, but my uncle went through something similar a couple of years ago. That's why I've been so calm about it compared to people who might know you better."

I took a deep breath as I carefully contemplated this idea. Not only did Kira not think I was insane, but I also wasn't the only person this had happened to. The thought both calmed and frightened me. I felt calmer knowing I wasn't some massive outlier in terms of a spiritual takeover, yet more terrified at the realization that the last case—her uncle's—seemingly had no resolution, at least as far as I knew at that point. Slowly, it dawned on me that the whole situation had just shifted. I wondered if her uncle had heard the same things I did, how long his sensations had lasted, and countless other questions that swirled in my mind driven by an eagerness for the truth.

Kira and I got up and walked out of the room and into the fresh air. As the sun rose, I instinctively covered my eyes, wary of any discomfort I had somehow grown accustomed to. For the first time in my college life, I had woken up somewhere other than my dorm. That might seem insignificant to some, but to me, it felt like progress. It wasn't as though Kira and I had done anything intimate, but being able to walk around before anyone else woke up left me with a memory I still haven't forgotten.

We wandered for a while, talking about general things in life and purposely avoiding the topic of what had happened. It wasn't that the truth didn't matter to us—it did—but I think we both silently agreed that we needed time to relax and distance ourselves from it.

As we strolled, though, I couldn't stop thinking about Kira's uncle. I know I said we were both trying to push it out of our minds, but I just couldn't do it. The memory of the night had impacted me so deeply that it felt more painful to try to forget it than to keep it at the forefront of my thoughts. Kira, on the other hand, seemed calm—probably because she had witnessed this kind of situation before. Still, she had never fully clarified what had happened to her uncle.

Eventually, we walked into a small café. I turned to her and asked, "Hey, Kira, so what happened to that uncle of yours? Like, did he just get over it, or could I talk to him about it?"

Immediately, I knew something was wrong. Her face fell, her expression turning dull and lifeless. She looked down as if preparing to tell me the worst news of my life. At the time, it honestly was.

Kira: "Yeah, Jesse, he, uh… died about a year later."

I could tell she didn't want to share this, but at the same time, I knew she wasn't lying—which scared me more than anything. I nodded, grabbed the coffee I had ordered, and sat back down in a state of shock. At that point, I didn't know what to think. Was I going to die in a year? Was Kira not telling me the whole story? I sipped my drink and pulled out my phone, desperate to research anything that might give me some hope.

Kira: "Jesse, he was sick at the time. I'm not saying the situation is or isn't the reason he died, but I'm just saying we have to be careful with what happened and how we resolve it."

I nodded in agreement. I didn't know if she thought saying that would calm me down or not. I just knew she couldn't bear the thought of lying to me at that moment, and I appreciated her honesty.

Kira and I talked for a while as we sipped our drinks. I kept asking her questions—about her life, what her uncle was like, and then... I lost my train of thought again. I leaned back in my chair, suddenly feeling the same tension return to my head.

Kira leaned over, trying to help me get up and out of the café, but I sat frozen, unable to move. Was it out of fear? I didn't know. All I knew was that the tension I had felt the night before was back, even though I thought it was over. It felt as though the entire restaurant could hear the uneven rhythm of my breathing. A small crowd of people started to gather around me.

As I sat there, lost in a dense state of shock, a tear rolled down my cheek, landing on the table just inches from the wet spot left by my coffee. Kira immediately realized something was wrong. She managed to help me out of the restaurant, shoving through the crowd and guiding me to a more concealed spot outside.

After a couple of minutes, my breathing began to steady, and I closed my eyes. Slowly, I felt my body returning to reality. When I opened my eyes, Kira was sitting next to me, her face filled with concern as she silently hoped I was okay.

I stood up cautiously, stumbling a little but feeling much better. Kira and I began to walk back to my dorm. I was grateful she didn't bring up what had just happened because, honestly, I felt I understood more about the events of the previous night than I did about the supposed relapse I had just experienced.

Kira: "Okay, Jesse, when you get some sleep, look up Dr. Jenkins using the contact info I'm going to send to your phone, all right? He's the guy who helped my uncle and someone who knows a lot more about this than any of us."

I replied with a soft "Okay," barely having the energy to unlock my apartment door. Once inside, I collapsed onto my bed, almost immediately falling asleep as I heard Kira close the door behind her on her way out.

That night, around seven pm., I woke up feeling more refreshed than I had in what felt like years. It was such a good feeling that, for a fleeting moment, I almost believed that the past 24 hours had been nothing more than a strange dream. As I sat up, I grabbed my phone from the floor where it had fallen and scrolled through my messages, remembering what Kira had told me before I passed out.

Kira: "Hey, Jesse. I hope you're feeling better. The doctor I mentioned is Dr. Jenkins, who is now Detective Colin Jenkins. I think it's best for you to contact him because of my repeated false alarms with him, but I recommend you look up some information about him before reaching out. I know he's usually busy, but I'm sure he'll help you. If you need anything, call me. Again, I hope you're feeling better.

P.S. Don't ask him about my uncle."

As I read the text, I felt a twinge of disappointment. Not just because it seemed like she was hiding something about her uncle and his claims, but also because of her tone. She was clearly worried about my health and genuinely cared, but I had hoped she felt the same connection between us that I did. Still, that was the least of my worries.

I walked over to my desk, determined to learn as much as I could about this Jenkins guy and his background. I researched for hours but found little beyond his impressive credentials as both a psychologist and a detective, along with some brief information about his upbringing. It felt like he had gone out of his way to keep people from knowing too much about him or his work.

I was on the verge of giving up, frustrated by the lack of information, when I clicked on what seemed to be a scammy website. That's where I found the truth—not just about Jenkins, but also about the uncle Kira had mentioned and the eerie connection to my own experience.

July 25, 1992

Today was the most interesting day at the job I had ever had. I found out that the case of Mr. Eli Whitts was one of demonic and supernatural nature. I stand here writing this as I have solved the mystery of what I have put all my life work into. This will be my last journal as the goal of my life Son this planet has been achieved. Mr. Whitts died 2 hours before I have written this due to a cause that I couldn't tell the public without being hung. I tried my best to document everything about him in the log below, but simply I don't know what to do from here. My goal of being in touch with the reality that we couldn't comprehend is now complete, as I will take the remainder of my life in studying these cases like Mr. Whitts, hoping I can save the next invaded brain from certain death from the voices beyond. From my journal, the journey has been fun but exhausting, and while death is sad, it is something that opens gates for the people who find the causes...

July 20, 1991- First encounter (voice to head)

July 28, 1991-Relapse before self-doubt.

November 18, 1991-What is causing this, a scream, a terror

November 26, 1991-A investigate the devil, a faith outlook

January 4, 1992-Mr. Whitts weak and damn near dead

May 3, 1992-Neice of Eli visits, seeming to know the truth

July 20, 1992- The last alive day of seeing Mr. Whitts, a man of trust in fate

I read the article over and over, unwilling to believe a single word of it. I didn't know what to think anymore. Part of me wished I had never found it, while another part of me knew it was fate that led me to it. Without hesitation, I printed the document, grabbed it, and ran outside to catch the metro, desperate to get to Kira as fast as I could. I texted her as I sprinted, letting her know I was on my way.

Was Kira more involved in this than I thought? What was Jenkins' real goal? Was I heading down the same path as her uncle? These questions swirled in my mind as I tried to piece it all together. I really believed any of it could be true.

I pulled out my phone and looked at the contact information Kira had given me. Without wasting time, I texted the number as I sat on the metro:

"Detective Colin Jenkins, this is Jesse. I am a student at Harvard Business School and would like to discuss a matter of demonic sensations I experienced earlier this week."

I had no idea how he would respond, but I didn't care. One way or another, I was going to uncover the truth—about myself, about Kira, and most importantly, about who Jenkins really was.

When the metro arrived at my stop, I jumped off and jogged the half mile to Kira's apartment. I knocked on her door impatiently, too anxious to wait any longer for answers.

Kira opened the door, but she looked irritated. "Look, Jesse, I get that you're going through this situation, but I already told you who to call—and it's freakin' midnight! You could've just called me instead of showing up."

"Sorry," I muttered, my mind racing with a million thoughts. I handed her the printed article and sat down on her couch.

"Kira, what can you tell me about this? Just tell me the truth. Please, Kira—that's the only thing I want from you right now."

Kira rolled her eyes as she looked over the printed page, her confusion deepening with every new word she read aloud. For the first time, I saw her unsure of what to say. Throughout high school and even now, she was always the first one to speak, always quick with her thoughts. I glanced at her repeatedly, waiting for her to say something, as I lay back on the couch, trying to make sense of everything.

Kira: "Okay, uh... yeah, this stuff is real. It's from Jenkins' journal, which was apparently written the day my uncle died. What I told you was true—my uncle was sick while he was going through all of this. As for Jenkins' goals or the journal itself, I never knew this even existed. My uncle found Jenkins through one of his friends when he was seeing him."

I looked at her, feeling a wave of doubt despite her explanation. "Promise me that's the truth. I can't handle any more lies in this situation. And second—did you just gloss over the part where he mentions a niece who, quote, 'seems to know the truth'?"

Kira nodded slowly, clearly processing everything I was pointing out.

Kira: "I know you want the truth as much as I do, Jesse. The niece he's referring to isn't me—it's my insane sister, who disappeared a couple of months ago. We can ask Jenkins about her. As far as my false alarms go, they were just about the weird things I noticed after my uncle passed. I was scared something similar might happen again, like a part two of that whole experience.

"Like... I don't think you understand what it was like being so close to not just my uncle but also my sister, who wouldn't stop going on about what she thought was causing all of it."

The only thing I wanted to do was scream at her—to yell at her for telling me I didn't understand what she had gone through when the last 24 hours of my life had been more surreal than anything she could've imagined. But I didn't. I knew I couldn't. Kira was the only person I trusted who didn't think I was insane.

"I texted him," I said as I got up and filled a cup of water from her faucet. "I don't know if I'll get a response, like you said, though." I sighed, setting the cup down and walking back over to her. "And, uh... I'm sorry about barging in. I'm just scared, and after finding nothing for hours, coming across such a catastrophic document wasn't exactly what I had in mind."

She paused for a moment before looking at me with a slight smile. "It's fine, Jesse. I need to sleep, in any case. You're, uh, welcome to stay the night—just relax, ok?"

I mouthed a "thank you" back to her as I pulled out my phone, scrolling aimlessly, trying to distract myself from the situation and the overwhelming stress that refused to let up. As the hours ticked toward early morning, my body began to relax. Feeling safe again, even briefly, was a relief in itself. A couple of hours later, I fell asleep—not for long, but just enough to feel rested when I woke up relatively early that morning.

It was now Sunday, and as I got up, the realization hit me. I walked over to Kira's computer, determined to email my professors and explain what had happened, hoping they'd give me some time off due to my unique situation. Just as I was about to hit "send," Kira caught sight of the email and stopped me.

Kira: "Jesse, do you really think one of them is not just going to believe you but also give you time off? I know you've got work and a hard school schedule, but do the assignments. I'll try to get in contact with Jenkins, okay?"

I nodded, thanking her for saving me from my impulsive decision. I turned my attention to my assignments, trying to push through, but about an hour in, I realized I wasn't going to get anything productive done. My mind was still racing. Frustrated, I switched my focus back to research—not about Jenkins this time, but about Kira's sister, someone I knew absolutely nothing about.

Two hours passed with no success. Finally, I stumbled upon her name in one of Kira's reports:

Nicole Whitts.

Nicole... Nicole... Where had I heard that name before? I racked my brain until it hit me. Will had told me something over the summer about an asylum he visited and a specific inmate confined there for her thoughts about the future and "supernaturalistic phenomena."

I jumped up from my seat and walked straight to Kira, barely registering how little thought I was putting into my actions.

"Hey, Kira, can we go visit Nicole? I think she can help us."

If I said she looked at me with a mix of fear and disgust, it would be an understatement.

Kira: "Are you *fucking crazy*, Jesse? I'm not even going to ask you how you know that name or where she is, but no, I'm not going to see her. You can do whatever you want, Jesse, but if you think you're mentally screwed up, you have no idea what you'd be walking into."

The more I thought about it, the more I regretted bringing up her sister. I didn't bother to apologize and just walked out of the room. My desperation for answers to the past was consuming me, causing me to disregard any relationships I had in the present. The craving for truth felt like an addiction—a need so strong that nothing else mattered.

I realized I wasn't going to stop until I spoke to Nicole, Kira, Jenkins, and anyone else who might hold a piece of the puzzle. I was willing to do whatever it took to find answers, especially if it meant avoiding the steps Jenkins had outlined in connection to Kira's uncle. If I were currently in the "questioning" phase, the next step would likely involve an outlook on faith and the devil—something I was determined to avoid at all costs.

But I didn't know how long to wait for Jenkins or how much trust to put in him when I didn't know a single thing about his true intentions.

Feeling a wave of hopelessness, I laid back down on the couch. Should I try to talk to Kira again? Should I go to Nicole? Or should I just abandon this chase before it even truly began?

As I closed my eyes, my phone buzzed. A text message from an unknown number lit up the screen:

"Hey, Mr. Jesse, I saw your text and would be interested in discussing your situation tonight at the town pier. I know you're scared, but trust me, your situation was solved before Mr. Owens."

CHAPTER 3
DETECTIVE COLIN JENKINS

"So, what you're telling me is the first text I get from this guy—a guy I was already kind of scared of—is some revealing message that proves this random person knows my last name?" For about the hundredth time in the past 24 hours, I sat back, completely unsure of who I was dealing with.

I was a Harvard student, a kid who had spent countless hours alone with my schoolwork or lost in thought, and yet, I don't think I had ever felt this much uncertantity in my entire life. It wasn't the act of thinking itself—I still loved that part—it was what I was thinking about that was draining me.

I got up and walked back to Kira's room, convinced she had to know more about this Jenkins guy than she was letting on.

"Kira, you have to be honest with me about this Jenkins guy. He said he's willing to help us, but how does he know my last name?"

Kira sighed, clearly frustrated but seemingly understanding my concerns.

Kira: "Okay, Jesse, I swear all I know is what I've already told you—about my uncle and, I guess, about my sister. But Jenkins doesn't share much about himself."

She paused, and for a moment, I thought she might kick me out of her room. Instead, she continued.

Kira: "Look, I get why you care so much. It is weird, and I can tell you what I know. But you have to promise me you won't go near Nicole or dig into her past."

I nodded and agreed. The only reason I wanted to talk to Nicole was to get answers. If Kira was going to give them to me, I figured there was no need to visit a literal mental asylum. I sat down at her desk, trying to give her the time and space to figure out how to explain everything.

All I could do was hope she would be honest with me. There was no way to prove if what she said was true, so I decided to trust her—just as she was trusting me.

Kira: "Okay, so basically, everything I told you earlier was true. The logs beneath the letter were events tied to my uncle and his situation. They were like a way for him to keep track of what happened in his specific case.

"My sister was the girl mentioned in the logs as the one who 'knew stuff.' What she knew… that's what got her sent to the mental hospital."

She sighed, her voice trembling as though she were about to burst into tears. I didn't want to see her cry, but I wasn't going to stop her from saying what I needed to hear.

Kira: "So, when Jenkins was dealing with my uncle, Nicole spiraled. She was even closer to him than I was, mostly because our dad really wasn't in the picture. Anyway, Nicole did her research—like you're trying to do—and she found evidence that basically claimed Jenkins was the one casting those voices. That's why you don't see much about him; he's practically erased himself from existence.

"I couldn't tell you if she was right. I couldn't even tell you if he really helped my uncle, Jesse. All I know is that Nicole spread her theory to anyone who would listen. That broke our relationship and eventually got her into trouble with the police."

I froze, unsure of what to say. My mind raced as I tried to process her words. Should I still meet with Jenkins? Should I try to forget everything I was hearing? Or should I go to the police to see if they knew anything?

As much as I wanted to give Kira some space, I knew one thing for sure: I couldn't ignore the sensations I had experienced.

"Kira? What do I do, however? What do *we* do? Do I respond to him or just let it play out?"

Kira: "I would wait to meet with him, Jess. You can respond if you want; don't act too desperate. And don't tell him it's not important—because, at this point, he knows it is."

I nodded, agreeing with her. If something else unexplainable happened, I'd meet with Jenkins out of desperation. But until then, I figured I'd wait and see how things unfolded.

Kira and I spent the rest of the day hanging out until I finally walked back to my apartment that evening, preparing for what now felt like the farthest thing from a normal week of school.

I didn't know if I'd have a relapse during class. I didn't know if that weekend would remain just a memory or become something permanent. I just didn't know.

That night, I sat at my desk, cramming homework like it was any other Sunday evening. But this wasn't a normal Sunday. It wasn't just my racing mind, consumed by thousands of worries about the voices. It was something else—hope.

It was strange. I should've felt worse than I ever had, but instead, I felt included, almost happier than I ever had. "Am I a terrible person for feeling happy after everything I've heard?" I didn't know—and honestly, I didn't care.

People always talk about the changes some experience in college, and for the first time, I was starting to feel it myself. I couldn't tell if it was a good change or not, or even one I wanted to happen, but I knew it was a change.

The next morning, I walked to class feeling completely normal—even refreshed. It was a new feeling, one I wasn't ready to let go of. I entered the classroom, took my seat in the back, and pulled out my books. I was more prepared than ever for a class I usually dreaded.

But ten minutes into the lecture, everything changed.

"Dead or alive, screams of death, a death of a teacher. Run, run—the echoes are real, Mr. Jesse Owens."

I froze, stumbling back in my seat, my mind racing. Kira wasn't here. Jenkins wasn't even a consideration at that moment. What was the voice saying? And was it *right*?

I scanned the room, my eyes darting across every corner, every crevice, every door. Paranoia consumed me as I tried to make sense of the situation. Before long, the entire class was staring—Jesse Owens was having a full-on mental breakdown in the middle of math.

I didn't want the attention. I didn't want the whispers, the laughter, or the concerned faces. I just wanted to *act*.

Before I knew it, I was standing at the front of the lecture hall, my voice trembling as I spoke words that probably landed Nicole in the asylum all those years ago: "Run. There's going to be a killing. And Mr. Cutler, you're the target."

The classroom erupted in chaos. Some students stared in disbelief, others laughed nervously, a few grabbed their phones, and a handful ran toward the exits. My teacher, visibly shaken, reached for his phone to call the authorities.

Then, a loud ring pierced the air.

I flinched, as did half the class. I looked up, first at the stunned faces of the students in front of me. But their expressions made it clear—something had happened.

I didn't know what they were looking at, but I knew one thing: I had to run.

I jumped up from my seat, stumbling a couple of times as I sprinted out of the classroom and into the streets. My head darted around like I was in a movie, scanning for anything familiar. Desperation guided my steps as I ran toward Kira's apartment. By some luck—or perhaps the sheer force of my will—I found her. She was outside her building with her small dog, looking as calm as ever.

As I ran up to her, drenched in sweat and out of breath, her face twisted in shock.

Kira: "Holy shit, Jesse! What happened? Okay, okay, you can go up to my place. It's apartment number 56."

Her concern was evident, but at that moment, I was just relieved she didn't hesitate to let me in. I jogged up to her apartment and collapsed onto the couch, my body shaking and soaked with sweat from both the sprint and the overwhelming stress.

A few minutes later, Kira came upstairs with a glass of water in hand. She set it on the table in front of me, her worried gaze fixed on mine as she turned on the TV.

Kira: "What happened, Jesse?"

I didn't know how to respond, so I stayed silent. My mind replayed the chaos from the classroom, the voices, the stares—it was too much to explain.

Kira flipped through the channels aimlessly until I saw something that made my stomach drop.

"Wait, Kira, stop!"

Kira: "What, Jesse? What's wrong? What channel?"

I pointed at the screen, my voice catching in my throat. She turned back to the news channel, and as I watched the scene unfold, my heart sank further into my chest.

The screen displayed my classroom, swarming with paramedics and police officers. Front and center in the frame was me, sitting on the floor next to an older man who appeared to be unconscious—or worse.

Kira and I sat frozen in silence, listening to the news anchor's voice narrate the surreal events of the morning:

"A bizarre story out of Harvard this morning. A screaming student, believed to be under the influence of drugs, predicted the death of his professor just minutes before it happened. Mr. Cutler was found dead shortly after from unknown causes. His body is

currently being examined at Massachusetts General Hospital. The student, who remains unidentified, is now being actively sought by the Cambridge Police Force."

As the words sank in, I turned to Kira, her face mirroring the shock I felt. My life, as I knew it, was over.

I lay back on the couch, more scared than I had ever been—scared of losing Kira, scared of the police, and terrified of what the investigation might uncover. To my surprise, however, Kira, who seemed more shocked than afraid, turned to me with an air of comfort rather than panic.

Kira: "Okay, first, we need to get out of here and on the road. Second, you need to text Jenkins with *exactly* the words I tell you. And third, you don't need to be arrested."

I sat up, looking at her with wide eyes, more surprised than before. "What do you mean, 'get out of here,' Kira? You want to run from the police? I didn't do anything wrong."

She nodded firmly. "Yes, because this same thing happened to my uncle, okay? Now, give me your phone and go pack the car."

I hesitated but ultimately had no other choice. I ran outside, grabbed a few clothes, her bag, and her dog's things, throwing them into her car. It wasn't like I ultimately agreed with her plan, but this was the first time she had ever mentioned her uncle in this much detail. Besides, what other option would I have had if I didn't trust her?

What I didn't know was what she was doing on my phone.

Kira was in the process of contacting Jenkins, which is something I probably wouldn't have agreed to. And honestly, she was right. I was desperate, but not enough to start trusting a guy with nothing to show for his past. I knew Kira had spoken to him a couple of times before, so if anyone was going to reach out to him, it should've been her. But still, I couldn't shake the feeling of uncertainty.

When she finally came out to the car about an hour later, I couldn't hold back my curiosity.

"Hey, before we leave, can you tell me why you took my phone for so long?"

Kira looked at me, giggled, and handed my phone back. "Go look for yourself, Jesse. It's exactly what you didn't want me to do if I'm being honest."

I immediately knew what she was talking about. As I opened my phone and read through the texts in the conversation, I felt a mix of confusion and surprise. For the first time, Jenkins was texting and acting like a normal person. But what stood out more was how well he seemed to understand Kira—far better than he understood me.

I couldn't tell if it was because I was so scared of what he might say or because Kira just knew how to talk to him after their past interactions. Either way, it was clear from the texts that Jenkins knew about what had happened earlier that day and was willing to help.

Kira: "So, yeah, honestly, he wasn't going to help you until this morning. He's been kind of skeptical about these cases ever since my uncle. But I guess what happened today was big enough to get his attention."

She laughed as she spoke, her tone a mix of annoyance and familiarity when talking about Jenkins.

Every time she laughed about this whole situation, I was confused. Sure, she had prior experience with these sensations, but I couldn't imagine myself ever laughing about it—even years later—if I managed to get through it.

Looking back on it, I realize that the car ride to meet Jenkins was one of the strangest emotional times of my life. It was mostly fear. Fear that my situation couldn't be fixed. Fear that I'd lose my scholarship. Fear that I'd lose my friends because of what had happened in the classroom.

The only thing keeping me focused was the knowledge that I *had* to figure out what was going on. I knew it was the only way to save my likely crumbling future at Harvard.

Kira and I didn't say much to each other during the drive, aside from a few exchanges about how to approach the doctor. Kira clearly understood how uncomfortable I was with him, but I think she also knew—as I did—that at least one meeting was necessary.

The only thing running through my mind, however, was the range of worst- and best-case scenarios for this encounter. The best-case scenario, I thought, was that he would immediately figure out what was wrong with me and simply tell me to get some rest. The worst-case scenario? I didn't even want to imagine it. The uncertainty of the situation terrified me. But deep down, what scared me most was knowing that the worst case—whatever it might be—was far more likely than the miracle outcome I had dreamed up.

The only reason I was going to this supposed doctor at all was because of Kira. Somehow, she trusted him, even though her uncle had died during their last interaction. All I knew about her uncle's story was what I had read in Jenkins' file, which was the main reason I barely trusted him—if at all.

When we pulled up to Jenkins' home, I was taken aback by how oddly normal it seemed. You'd think someone like him would live in a secretive, off-the-grid location, but no—his house was a simple one-story condo in the middle of an average neighborhood.

At that point, I didn't know what to think. Was Jenkins just a regular guy with a genuine desire to help? Or was there something more sinister lurking beneath the façade of the tidy house and trimmed grass? I couldn't tell, but I knew I had to give him a chance, if not for myself, then at least for Kira's sake.

Kira and I walked up to the door. While I glanced around nervously, scanning for anything out of place, Kira seemed calmer than ever. The sound of heavy footsteps approached the door, and my stomach knotted in anticipation.

Jenkins: "Oh, hello, Kira... and you must be Jesse, right?"

I nodded, my nerves betraying me as I tried to make sense of how normal this man seemed.

I had heard stories about people who, after experiencing so much fear, became almost immune to it. But meeting someone who fits that description in real life was nothing short of shocking.

Jenkins: "Right. Yeah, come in. Your story is very real, if I may say so myself—probably the worst case I've dealt with since Kira's uncle."

Kira looked at him with a strange expression, almost like an old friend who had betrayed her—but without the anger, just something unspoken lingering beneath the surface.

As we walked in, I scanned the space, still not feeling entirely safe. When I sat down in the living room, all I could think about were the hundreds of questions swirling in my mind and the answers I desperately wanted.

Jenkins: "Help yourself to anything you need, Jesse. I just want to get some background from Kira before we dive into your case."

"Yeah, okay, take your time, sir."

That statement brought me a slight sense of relief. It not only gave me time to think about what I wanted to tell him and how I was going to approach the conversation, but it also allowed me to look around discreetly, hoping to learn something about this enigmatic man who seemed to thrive in anonymity.

As Kira and Jenkins stepped into another room, I stood up, quietly exploring. To this day, I still don't know whether I was relieved or disappointed, but I didn't find much. Aside from a couple of locked cabinets and an old door that likely led to the basement, everything else seemed normal.

Was Jenkins just a regular guy with an unusual expertise in spirits? I didn't know, but I had to talk to him. And with time running out, I still wasn't sure what I was going to say.

As I sat back down, something caught my eye— Kira's phone lighting up with a notification. A text. From Nicole, Kira's imprisoned sister.

My heart raced. Looking around frantically to make sure no one would catch me, I unlocked her phone using her birthday as the password. I navigated to the texts, desperate to uncover what my only friend at the time wasn't telling me.

The conversation seemed normal at first. They talked about life, my situation, their uncle in small fragments, and Jenkins—something I immediately focused on.

As I scrolled further, I noticed a heated discussion about Jenkins. It appeared to be an argument between the two sisters about whether or not to trust him with my case. Surprisingly, Kira was the one who didn't think it was a good idea to involve him. While she didn't fully explain her reasoning in the texts, it clearly stemmed from what had happened with their uncle.

What confused me even more was how Kira had told me that Nicole didn't trust Jenkins at all. And yet, now Nicole seemed to be advocating for him in my case.

I put the phone down just in time, still processing what I had read as Jenkins and Kira walked back into the room, sitting on either side of me. I glanced at Kira, then at Jenkins, before finally speaking.

"Before we discuss my case, I need to know what happened with Kira's uncle."

Both of them sighed, leaning back in their chairs. Kira opened her mouth to speak, but Jenkins immediately cut her off.

Jenkins: "Okay." He paused as if debating whether to lie, but he seemed to realize I would probably be able to tell if he did. "So, what do you know before I say anything?"

I hesitated, glancing at Kira. Should I mention the journal? Her blank stare gave nothing away, so I decided it was better to lie than to risk alarming Jenkins with the sight of such a document.

"Tell me as if I don't know anything, sir, except that his case was similar to mine."

Jenkins sat up straighter, his eyes scanning me briefly before he began.

Jenkins: "His case wasn't as similar to yours as you might think. Mr. Whitts was a fine man, much older than you and even more terrified at the time. I first met Mr. Whitts at a space conference about a year before his initial encounter. I was brought in later by a fellow doctors who couldn't make progress due to his own fears."

For the next ten minutes, Jenkins explained his relationship with Mr. Whitts, the details of the first and second encounters, and how they had tried to cope with the episodes. My description might seem slim, but Jenkins had a practiced way of withholding just enough to keep me guessing. Whether he was lying, I couldn't tell, but I knew I had one more question to ask before my case could be brought up.

"So, Mr. Jenkins, in a disclosed document, it states that you solved his case but, quote, couldn't share the answer without being hanged. What does that mean?"

Jenkins' expression shifted to one of distress while Kira looked down, her disappointment almost palpable.

Jenkins: "Yeah, uh... I don't know where you heard that from, but yeah. His death was kept hidden from the public for a while, even from Kira, because of the evidence tied to it. Here's a picture if you really want to understand what I'm talking about—and why we need to start your case immediately."

He handed me a picture of Mr. Whitts. The image was horrifying. The man looked utterly devoid of happiness, humanity, or anything normal. His face bore near-zero traces of earthly life, save for a few scars etched across his skin.

The picture was unlike anything I had ever seen before. I put the phone down, my heart pounding faster than I could ever remember, as the terrifying thought crossed my mind: was this my fate?

"Wait... so, what... What happened to him, sir? Am I on the same path?"

Jenkins chuckled softly as he took his phone back. "Oh no, Mr. Whitts was cursed for years prior to his episodes. From what Kira has told me, anything physical you're experiencing is just your body's response to what you hear. I have to say, though, I've never had a case involving tremors that could seemingly predict death."

He leaned forward slightly, his tone growing more serious. "Why don't we start there, Mr. Owens? Tell me about what happened this morning."

As terrified as I was to relive the pain, Kira's hand around mine gave me just enough strength to begin. I took a deep breath and gave a brief explanation.

"Yeah, so... I was in class like any other day. I went to turn in my test, and then... everything went wrong."

I could feel my head clouding with darkness as I replayed the morning's events in my mind.

"So, I got up there, and I immediately fell. Honestly, I don't even remember what I said—it's probably on tape. Anyway, I looked to my right afterward, and my teacher was on the ground, covered in his own blood. But it was strange—there were no scars, no gunshots—just blood. And I ran out."

Kira looked at me, confusion evident on her face. She hesitated before speaking, her voice unsteady.

"Jesse, you told me you heard a scream and ran— nothing about blood."

"Yeah." I nodded, glancing back at her. "I didn't see any blood—well, not when I was there. Once I got back to your place, we watched the news while you packed. I saw it then."

It was as if Jenkins could sense that I wasn't being entirely truthful, likely out of fear of scaring Kira further. He turned to her and gently instructed her to step outside and wait in the car for a bit.

Kira agreed, albeit reluctantly, and left the room. As she closed the door behind her, Jenkins turned back to me, his eyes fixed on my trembling, guilt-ridden self.

Jenkins: "If I'm going to help you, Jesse, I need to know everything—not just the surface details."

I sighed, still unsure if I could fully trust him. But at this point, I had already confessed to some kind of murder—or at least something close to it—so what did I really have to lose?

"Yeah... so, I didn't see it on the news. When I was running back to Kira's, I tripped over a stump on the sidewalk and fell into another trance. This one only lasted a few seconds. The only thing I saw before I woke up was my professor's body, covered in blood, and my hand over it—also dripping red—with no evidence of whose remains it actually was."

Jenkins froze for a moment before getting up. He walked over to one of the locked cabinets I had noticed earlier, retrieving a hidden notebook.

Jenkins: "Okay. My advice to you is this: write down everything you know, then focus on living your life with Kira. Stay out of public places, especially anywhere that reminds you of home. I can't help you unless I know every single encounter you've had—even if it was just a second of uneasiness in the past two weeks."

I nodded reluctantly, taking the notebook from him. I wanted to flip through the pages first, but I knew that doing so would only confirm my worst fears.

The next 30 minutes of my life were spent writing down every detail I could recall—everything from where I had woken up each morning to the six episodes I had endured. Some had lasted minutes, while others had been brief seconds, like the one from earlier that day.

When I finished, I stood up, my breathing slower but still heavy with uncertainty. Despite following his instructions, I didn't completely trust this so-called detective.

"So, what now?" I asked, grabbing my bag from the floor.

Jenkins: "Now you wait. Have Kira call me if anything else goes wrong, but otherwise, expect a call from me in the next few days. I'll talk to a couple of people on my end. And don't worry—we'll solve this before it's too late."

The devious smile that spread across his face wasn't exactly reassuring, but for some reason, I believed him.

I walked out to Kira's car, hoping—praying—that it would be the last time I'd have to see Jenkins. Kira and I drove off, but where to? Neither of us had any idea.

All that was clear was this: I couldn't go anywhere near that school, and Kira wasn't planning to leave me behind.

The next couple of days were uneventful, almost maddeningly so. Kira and I split hotel bills, grabbed food, completed our work through online networks, took care of her dog, and sat in silence, waiting for a call from Jenkins.

It wasn't that we didn't like talking to each other or that we didn't have feelings for each other. It just felt like the mood was never right to speak about the future—whether in terms of us or our careers. As much as I knew Kira cared about me, I couldn't help but wonder why she was so willing to drop everything in her life to help me, reconnecting with a case tied to her late uncle.

I was too scared to ask her, though—not because I thought she'd leave, but because I knew she wouldn't. I knew that if I told her what I had seen on her phone, it would only deepen her involvement with Jenkins. She would care even more about everything he did, whether I wanted her to or not.

After a few days of this monotonous waiting, I couldn't take it anymore. I decided to call Jenkins. The longer I waited for answers, the more likely it seemed that another episode would occur—one that would push me even closer to my eventual breakdown.

To my surprise, Jenkins picked up immediately. His first words were filled with concern.

Jenkins: "Jesse, are you okay? Are you hurt?"

Jesse: "No, I'm fine, detective. I was just wondering if there's been any update—or if there's anything I can do to help."

I'll admit it: I was terrified. I tried to stay calm, but my trembling voice probably gave me away. Jenkins could tell I wasn't in a good place.

Jenkins: "I do have an idea, but I doubt you're going to believe it. In short, it seems like someone from your past may have come into contact with some kind of unknown auditory interference—something I can't say I've ever dealt with before."

I froze, processing his words as my anxiety skyrocketed. I glanced around for Kira, but she wasn't there. Panic set in, and I bolted from the hotel, my heart pounding harder than ever. Each beat seemed to radiate through my chest, overwhelming me until I collapsed to the ground once again.

CHAPTER 4
A VOICE OR A STORY

Luckily for me, I woke up almost immediately, not experiencing any sensations while I was out—which was as surprising as it was relieving. As I got up, with Kira's help (she had apparently seen what had happened), I glanced at her. I didn't say anything, but the look we exchanged was enough to acknowledge that she was still there for me.

Kira: "Hey Jess, I think you're fine. It just seems like a panic attack, but we should probably take you to a hospital."

I stared at her, confused. Had she forgotten everything that had happened over the past week?

"Kira, I can't go to the hospital. I need to stay away from Harvard for now—at least until we figure out what happened that morning."

As much as I struggled to trust her after what I had seen on her phone, I had no choice but to rely on her. The fear of being alone in all of this was far worse than my doubts about her. Despite my lingering worries, I knew she was the only thing keeping me from completely losing my mind over the sensations I had experienced.

We got back into her car and began driving away from the hotel. The silence between us felt heavy. I wanted to ask her about Nicole, but I couldn't bring myself to say anything yet. It wasn't the right time.

We drove for over an hour, and as much as I tried to converse with her normally, I couldn't. The thought of what I'd seen on her phone kept nagging at me. I turned to her, pausing before finally speaking.

"Kira, we need to talk about something—something that's been on my mind constantly for the past hour."

Kira glanced at me briefly, her tone cautious but light.

Kira: "Yeah, what is it, Jesse? And if it's about our relationship, we're just friends, so..."

I exhaled slowly, partly baffled by why that would be the first thing to come to her mind and partly annoyed that she didn't seem to feel the same connection I did.

"Look, when you were talking to Jenkins earlier, your phone buzzed—with a text... a text from Nicole. You know, the sister you said was in a mental clinic."

Kira looked at me in shock, slamming on the brakes and pulling over to the side of the road. Her expression was a mix of anger and disappointment.

"I need you to tell me you didn't open my phone," she demanded. "What happened with my sister and where she is now is none of your business, Jesse."

I sighed, feeling the weight of her words. "I can't lie to you, Kira. I looked at your texts with her, and I need some answers. I need to know where she is. I need to talk to Nicole. And most importantly, I need to know why you let me go to Jenkins when you didn't even think he was reliable."

Kira nodded slowly, her expression unreadable. She said only, "Okay, fine. I'll drive you there."

She looked disappointed, but it was as if a weight had been lifted from her shoulders. Maybe she knew I was bound to meet Nicole eventually, and this moment was inevitable.

As I sat back in my seat as she started driving, a sense of regret settled in. The smallest part of me, however, still felt like this was something I *had* to do.

"I'm sorry," I said, my voice soft. "I really am. I wasn't going to say anything, but it spooked me. I trusted you, Kira, and you lied about her, so…"

Kira turned to me briefly, her face filled with shock as a tear rolled down her cheek. When she spoke, her tone was sharp—angrier than I'd ever heard her.

"What the hell do you mean, 'trusting me'? We've known each other for two weeks, Jesse! And now you think it's okay to go through my phone to pry into my *fucking* sister's life? Nicole was *destroyed* when Eli died. So yeah, I'm sorry if you feel offended, but I didn't lie about Nicole. And once you meet her, you'll understand why I didn't want you to talk to her or Jenkins about your sensations."

Her words stung. I wasn't surprised she was yelling—I deserved that—but what struck me most was how emotional she was. She seemed to blame me for trying to piece together my own case.

Looking back on it now, I can admit I was being an idiot. But at the time, the only thing I cared about was figuring out why and how I was feeling this overwhelming terror. Even as she yelled, I mentally justified my actions. I told myself that anyone in my situation would have done the same. It was selfish, sure, but in the moment, I gave myself a pass.

The rest of the 30-minute drive to Nicole's residence at the closest facility was awkward, to say the least. I didn't want to say anything that might make Kira hate me more than I already thought she did. The feeling was eerily similar to the night we first met, and that scared me—not just because I didn't want to relive that night and everything that had happened, but also because I had hoped it would be the last time I ever felt out of place with Kira.

As we parked, we moved in silence, avoiding each other's gaze while stepping out of the car and looking around the facility.

I knew, however, that the worst thing we could do was approach Nicole without being on speaking terms ourselves. I decided to break the silence.

"Kira, wait. I know I screwed up, but I've never been here before. If I'm going to trust you with this whole facility process, I need you to talk to me."

Kira sighed; her expression with a mix of reluctant agreement and lingering frustration.

"Yeah, Jesse. Look, just follow my lead, and once we talk to her, let me handle the conversation. We won't fight about it. Okay?"

I nodded, following her into the facility, my eyes scanning the unfamiliar surroundings. The main hall resembled a hospital, but it carried an unsettling, eerie aura. The pristine white walls and floors offered no comfort, the only splash of color being the desk that stood starkly in front of us.

The silence was broken only by shrieks—not the distant echoes I had heard weeks ago, but present, immediate, and disturbingly close, as though they came from the rooms around us.

Kira handled the check-in and led us down the hall toward Nicole's room. She started explaining things about Nicole, including details and rules I needed to follow during our visit.

I wish I could say I listened to everything she said, but the truth is, I barely caught any of it. The closer we got to Nicole's room, the more regret began to set in.

Fear crept over me as I considered the possibility that, if I didn't figure out what was happening to me, this facility could one day become my home—my cage. The thought of being trapped here, forced to admit to something I didn't even fully understand, was unbearable.

We reached her room a little while later, but before we entered, I nervously grabbed Kira's shoulder. Like so many things I had done over the past week, I didn't know why—I just knew it was the only way to get her attention in such a tense moment.

Kira: "What the hell, Jesse? Something wrong with your elaborate plan?"

I nodded, struggling to put my fears into words without proving her point. I knew I still had to see Nicole, but I was terrified of what might happen. As fascinating as she seemed through Kira's stories, those stories were all I knew. I had no idea what condition she was in, what had landed her in this place, or why she was so against Jenkins and my case.

"I'm fine, Kira. Just nervous, I guess."

Kira nodded, then knocked on the door. When the light above it turned green, she opened it and walked in.

Kira: "Hey, sis. Long time."

Nicole lay in the bed, looking frail and sickly, yet she resembled Kira so much it startled me. The long dark hair, the tiny freckles, the faint yet familiar smile—it was uncanny. She looked so much like the girl I had grown close to that it felt as though I had dodged a bullet.

"Uh... hi," I stammered, my voice barely above a whisper. I didn't know what to say. Meeting her for the first time, combined with my nerves, turned my words into a mess of gibberish.

Nicole sat up slowly, yawning softly before glancing around the room. Her eyes fixed on me.

Nicole: "So, you must be the problem kid," she said in an almost ominous tone. "And you're here because my sister couldn't help you? Or am I missing something?"

Kira rolled her eyes, her irritation visible. It seemed like there was something she wanted to say, but she held back as if eager to leave rather than prolong the moment.

Kira: "No, Nicole. Well, yes—he's that kid. But no, we're here because he wants to talk to you about our uncle. He saw our texts."

Nicole smirked faintly, her tone dripping with sarcasm as she replied.

Nicole: "Oh, you mean the texts where you insisted on trusting the detective who nearly ruined my life? The one who killed our uncle? And for what? Because he set you up with his so-called 'clear' deception?"

I looked at Kira, then at Nicole, in shock. "Wait, what happened? What do you mean, *killed your uncle*? I saw the journal! And how did he deceive Kira? I'm here to get my questions answered—not to have more of them."

Nicole laughed, a sharp, unsettling sound that echoed through the room. It was almost as though she *wanted* to seem unhinged.

Nicole: "Kira didn't tell you anything, did she? That journal was written *after* my uncle died—and after she called the cops on me, just to get me back."

I leaned back against the wall across from the bed, her words sinking in. Was I trusting the wrong person? How much more was Kira hiding from me? Questions swirled in my mind, but I forced myself to stay quiet. Kira had told me to let her lead the conversation, so for now, I tried to hold back.

Kira: "Look, sis, we just need your help. You can ridicule me or whatever you want *after* you help Jesse."

Nicole sighed, her posture relaxing slightly. She seemed to actually consider helping us, which was more surprising at the moment than it seems in hindsight.

Nicole: "Yeah, fine. What do you want to know? I don't have much time with you both anyway."

Kira and I both nodded. Then she looked at me, her expression softening slightly as if to give me permission to ask the questions that were racing through my mind.

"Okay," I began slowly, carefully choosing my words. I was starting to understand how sensitive this topic was. "Why didn't you want me to go to Jenkins? I had to go to somebody, right?"

Nicole: "Well, yeah. But as much as Jenkins figured out our uncle's case, he equally dismissed any evidence I tried to provide him. It was like he was always hiding something. Even when Eli died, he never told me how. All he said was that he wrote about it and that Eli died peacefully".

"That's why I told Kira not to take you there. If there's one thing Jenkins excels at, it's deception and mistrust. Giving him any satisfaction only plays into his hands."

I slid down the wall, sitting against it, more confused than ever. My gaze dropped to the floor, my thoughts swirling, each one heavier than the last. "Wait... but how did he deceive you? If Kira was the one who admitted you, how was Jenkins involved beyond providing the conclusions about Eli's death?"

Nicole nodded as though she understood she was speaking to someone with no experience dealing with Jenkins and his secrets.

Nicole: "Okay. After Eli died and was buried, I..." She paused, sighing deeply, her voice strained. It felt like she was addressing Kira more than me. "I dug up his grave. And when I did, I found multiple lacerations on his face and skull. It was almost like his body had been tampered with—like his post-mortem state was being investigated."

Before I could respond, Kira collapsed, almost fainting. I caught her just in time as tears streamed down her face. She picked herself back up, trembling.

"What did you do?" she asked Nicole, her voice cracking. "And what—do you think Jenkins unburied him? Stole his corpse to figure out what really happened? And I'm guessing you think he killed him too?"

Nicole shook her head violently. "No, no, I *know* Jenkins didn't kill him. But I *do* think he messed with the body. And call me crazy all you want, Kira, but I have proof."

Nicole's gaze turned to me, sharp and unyielding as she continued. "I don't know how you found that journal entry, but I have the rest of it—the rest of Jenkins' findings once he had the body."

Nicole walked over to one of the few cabinets in the room, reached down, and pulled out a crumpled ball of aged, tanned paper. She handed it to me with a stern look.

Nicole: "There. Read that—both of you. Then, you can ask me again why I didn't want you to get involved with Jenkins. As trustworthy as he seems—and while he *might* be able to solve your case before your inevitable disappearance—he isn't someone I'd recommend to anyone I remotely cared about."

Before I could take the crumpled sheet, Kira snatched it from Nicole's hand.

Kira: "How do we even know he wrote this? No more lies, sis. I need the *fuckin'* truth. Was this the next page?"

As Nicole nodded sincerely, the crumpled paper slipped from her grasp, landing limply in my hand. I hesitated for a moment, not knowing what I would find—but honestly, at that point, I didn't care either way.

When I opened it, however, the contents shocked me. What I read would prove to be more helpful than I expected, but it would also haunt a part of my existence every day until this divine misery was resolved.

August 5, 1993

I know I said the journal I wrote as a conclusion to the death and passing of my former client, Eli Whitts, would be my final goodbye. But, to my surprise, I have decided to write one final entry about my life of mystery.

I have not been entirely honest with any of my peers. My life, too, was infected by the same demons I now investigate—a situation I endured years ago and spent every day since trying to forget.

Last month, I wrote an admission to a crime of unburial. This is not something I had ever done before. But when it came to Mr. Whitts, it was impossible for me to continue my life without a sense of closure.

After committing such an offense, I proceeded to make certain indentations on the subject's skin, uncovering traces of infected bacteria and a disassociated pattern in his brain waves. I can conclude that this person's death was not caused by the demons that haunted him but rather by a rare disease I had been unaware of when questioning Mr. Whitts.

His death still haunts me, especially with the thought of his two nieces:

One, a girl of incredible intelligence, deemed psychotic—a girl with ideas I chose to dissuade because of my own past experiences.

The other, a girl of great beauty, seemingly God's creation, who became the subject I entrusted to keep my secret safe as I conducted my tests on their uncle.

Once again, however, this will be my final entry. This is an entry to hopefully conclude the life of true mystery I have wasted due to my own superstitions.

As novelist Wei Hui states, *"Crazy people are considered mad by the rest of society only because their intelligence isn't understood."*

To anyone brave enough to endure such endeavors, I wish you luck. But I leave you with this warning: constant distress will follow.

Goodbye.

Trusted Detective – Colin Brussels Jenkins

As I read each word aloud, the tension in the room thickened. I finally understood why Kira and Nicole had such differing views on Jenkins. Jenkins had used Kira—not knowingly on her part, of course—but he had still manipulated her, using her as a pawn in his desperate attempt to escape the misery of his own life.

And then there was Nicole, the brilliant niece Jenkins had intentionally ignored, likely because she reminded him of someone—or perhaps something—

from his past. Despite Nicole's sharp mind and determination, Jenkins had dismissed her, leaving her to wrestle with truths he refused to acknowledge.

In the end, I realized my own words only held so much weight. What I truly needed were the opinions of both Kira and Nicole before deciding whether to return to Jenkins for help.

Kira: "Wow… uhm… sorry, Nicole. I… I didn't know about that. It doesn't change what you did, but honestly, I feel like Jesse should go to Jenkins more than anything now."

Nicole: "Look, I agree he needs to be involved. I'm just saying, don't rope him into the same situation I was in just because of your anger toward the guy. Jesse seems like a good guy, and putting him alone with Jenkins to chase something that hasn't come up in almost three years… it's not right."

Before either of them could say more, I stood up, looking at both of them.

"I need to know what happened with you two. It's obviously tied to Jenkins, but I don't know how. And as sensitive as it might be, I think it's the key to understanding what I'm dealing with."

They both hesitated. Nicole nodded first, but Kira took longer to agree.

Nicole: "Look, sis, he needs to know. He's right, and it's the reason you're so invested in helping Jenkins in the first place."

Kira: "I know you're right. But... I honestly don't know if I can trust him enough with something so personal."

Nicole: "Then leave, Kira. I'll tell him what happened—with you, with Jenkins, and whatever other truths you've been hiding from the guy you claim to care about."

Kira sighed, clearly torn. After a moment, she looked at me, her resolve softening.

"Okay," she said, her voice low as she struggled with the decision. "Where do I even start?"

And then she began to explain everything.

Why was Nicole in this facility?

Why did Kira resent her so deeply?

And why, of all people, had Jenkins been chosen in the first place?

CHAPTER 5
NICOLE JASMINE WHITTS

It was May 3rd, 1992, the first day I met Mr. Jenkins. My sister Kira was out of town for the day with some friends of hers, which wasn't surprising given the situation. If nothing else, I had learned that every time a difficult situation arose, my sister would disappear for weeks, seemingly not caring to help or even, in this situation, provide for our uncle, who was closer to dying than anything. As uneventful as the situation was due to their seemingly being no cure, it would have been nice to have my sister by my side as I visited. This wasn't the first time she had done such a thing. Kira had gone on something she described as a "spiritual journey" when our parents passed. The time surrounding it was obviously heartbreaking for me, so knowing Kira was in Europe instead of at her own parents' funeral was slightly disturbing, to say the least.

As I got ready that morning, I was nervous to meet a man who, according to Kira, was not only a genius but the only man in the world who could deal with the sounds and feelings my uncle had heard. Most of me didn't even want to go, but I loved my uncle Eli more than anything, so I knew I had to go and see the detective for his sake.

Once I got to Jenkins's, I was immediately skeptical. For a guy who was a supposed genius and mastermind with such complex elements, his house and living situation seemed relatively simple, rather poor for a man of his caliber. I knocked on his door, still half regretting the idea of even coming to such a place, but before I could even contemplate such a thought, I was welcomed in by a tall, bespectacled man who seemed equally as charming as Kira described.

Jenkins and I walked in, sitting down in his living room. I think he could tell I was nervous with my demeanor as he spoke softly, asking if I wanted a drink. "Uh, I'm okay, sir," I replied softly, in a state of nervous shock, again not really knowing anything besides the slivers of description I took from Kira's texts.

Jenkins: "So, Kira's sister, right?" he stated as he sat down across from me. "As beautiful and smart as advertised, and uhm, sorry about the loss of Mr. and Ms. Whitts. Your parents were lovely people."

I nodded. "Thanks, but I'm only here to help with my ill uncle's case, Detective." The last thing I wanted was a bad first impression with the man who could save my uncle, but at the same time, I didn't really have time to flirt with a 30-year-old man. Jenkins smiled. His smile reminded me so much of my dad that I felt a calming presence when he would do so. He continued to speak softly as he talked about my uncle's background, quickly explaining all I would need to know when it came to my sister's interactions with him.

"Thanks," I said as he finished his spoken introduction. "Honestly, I have ideas about the result you're trying to come to, but I can only share them if I know that you are 100 percent the man that my sister trusts."

Jenkins: "Look, I don't think I can say anything that will completely gain your trust on this night. All I can say, however, is that your father is how I knew about your family prior to our meeting, and he's the only reason I'm alive today. So whatever you say, if you think it will really help his brother, then I am willing to hear you out, Nicole."

I nodded, looking up at him. I didn't know why I trusted him, but I did enough to take the next hour to explain the remainder of my thoughts when it came to the source of these apparent voices. "When looking at the report that you gave my uncle, I realized a case of mistype when it comes to his voices. When I last talked to him, he discussed the different versions of sensations in segments of screams, but they were older, pitched ones. Not only that, but his last background check done through his MRI reported dislodged brain waves. I'm not saying you're incorrect, sir, but I think that you are simply exaggerating this case because of a personal effect."

Jenkins stood up, pacing around the room with immense speed, almost in a run, seeming to try to find the right words to say to me, an average girl who had figured out exactly why my uncle was still being investigated.

Jenkins: "Look, even if you were the tiniest bit right, why would I ever endanger someone I care about so much just so my name gets out? I did have such an experience during the dark times in my life, and that wasn't some medical procedure. The doctor who looked at my case destroyed the chance of my life ever being normal again. So while your findings might be right, they aren't going to be the result of death for your uncle."

I sat back on the couch, more shocked than anything at the words that had just come out of his mouth. I just couldn't figure out why Kira was such an advocate for this guy who seemed to be anything but trustworthy. The only thing I wanted to do was get out of there, but until I knew precisely what Jenkins was doing with my uncle, I needed to stay. "I didn't mean to offend you, okay? My sister trusts you a lot, and I'm trying to figure out why."

Jenkins sighed as he looked at me up and down. It almost seemed like, for the first time in a while, someone had gotten personal with him, questioning him on a topic that he seemed optimistic to an experienced genius on. "Yeah, yeah. Your uncle is safe; he's in a hospital right now, and my conversations with him have been very influential. Not only is the man a brilliant individual, but his insight into what he has heard is near impossible."

I sat back. I was so confused about what the issue really was with my uncle, but again, I needed to know why my sister trusted him so much when he just didn't seem all that reliable. "So why does Kira like you so much?" I asked with a calm voice, trying not to make him as nervous as before.

Jenkins: "Your sister and I have been conversing for a while. We have made some deals and have also talked about your uncle's process through the minute details of his past life. If she didn't trust me as much as I trusted her, it wouldn't work, and your uncle wouldn't be as close as he is to survival."

I nodded, not wanting to say anything more to such a mysterious man. I got up, shook his hand, and bolted out of the house as quickly as I came in. I still had no idea what type of supposed deal he was doing with my sister or if he was even helping my uncle, but I had talked to him, against my own desires, just for Kira, who was nowhere to be seen.

Honestly, the next couple of weeks, I didn't think much of it. I had talked to Kira a couple of times in those weeks after she had returned, but the conversations normally turned into high-pressured arguments that most sisters wouldn't have. She kept saying how she was visiting Jenkins, and for some reason, I would always take those comments with a grain of salt. The last thing I wanted to assume was that my sister was having some type of affair with such a crazy man, but again, I really didn't know her too well. I mean, yeah, we were sisters, but every time any other pair of siblings would go through something, they would do it together, not us though.

For some reason, however, the constant disconnect we had just seemed normal. We were so different from the moment we were born that I would have been more confused if we had become inseparable. Kira was always an outgoing girl who trusted anything and anyone who gave her hope. I was damn near the opposite. I was a person who placed my trust in nearly nothing due to my past and, and I was someone who always tried to solve things like this on my own. Looking back on it, if I had just looked at my sister, looked at Jenkins, and stopped the process and things he was doing... The possibilities of outcomes for not just myself but for our now-dead uncle were endless. I knew for a fact that he didn't have anything demonic happening. Well, maybe he did. But the reason he died was due to those lacerations, not because some demon infected his brainwaves.

Kira and my relationship stayed near the same for the next couple of days. We would occasionally talk about once a day when she would explain to me about her and Jenkins' conversations, which honestly got weirder and weirder. They went from talking about my uncle to talking about Jenkins' life to talking about the future of such spirits. And while I tried to convince Kira to stop meeting up with him, it almost became a sort of addiction for her.

I never could find out why until about a week later when I was told to meet up with her and Jenkins one last time. As soon as her text came through, my first response was a phrase that stated how "it was the last thing I wanted to do and that I didn't trust the supposed detective at all." Luckily for me, though, that wasn't the last text. Kira and I continued to argue in the text back and forth for the next 30 minutes before I finally gave in, agreeing to meet up with them back at the Jenkins' residence. After I agreed, I got ready, deciding to bring a small recording device in case I heard anything in a conversation that was destined to be about as far from reality as possible.

I drove over to the house and walked in, and I immediately felt like something was off. Jenkins and Kira were sitting on the couch next to each other like they were long-lost friends, and then there was me, standing across from them in a mental state comparable to most of the people that I currently reside with.

"So, what's going on, why are we here? And why was it so important?"

Kira knew me well enough to tell when I wasn't in the mood to discuss much of anything, so she babbled as she heard me finish my thoughts. "Jenkins wanted to come clear to both of us and explain the state of our uncle that I... have been trying to explain to your deflected mind."

Jenkins: "Okay, be nice, Kira. Your sister is right, though, so please sit down so you can leave as quickly as your emotions prescribe."

I looked at both with a sense of disgust, but hearing that I might finally get the truth out of such a mysterious so-called detective gave me just enough motivation to want to stay. "Fine," I said as I sat down across from them, turning my device on from behind my bag. "But if I don't hear the truth, I'm leaving... any more of this demonic your uncle was chosen shit, and I'm gone."

Jenkins looked at me, nodding. It seemed to be the first time he ever looked at me with a face, knowing I was 100% serious about everything I said. "Okay, first off, you're right about the lacerations. We had an undisclosed MRI done, and they had an affect. But that doesn't mean I wasn't right. Unless your uncle was in a war, which I know for a fact he wasn't, those brain waves were affected by something in Kira and my opinion to be supernatural."

I laughed to myself as he finished talking. "Kira, don't tell me you believe this guy. A demon, a sound... invaded our uncle's brain and is killing him?" I nodded. "Okay, I'm going to take my uncle out of the hospital and take him to a real doctor, okay?"

Kira looked at me in shock. The way she looked at me was like I had never said anything remotely intelligent before. "Nicole, you must believe us. There's too much evidence to prove that we are right.

A new doctor will do nothing about the main problem and it will kill him. If he dies, we are done. FOREVER."

Jenkins sat there, almost admiring everything Kira said. He looked at her and then at me as I thought about what path I was going to take. "Fine, Kira, but if he dies, dies because your *dear* detective guy won't medically treat him... I won't just be charging your friend with murder."

I got up as soon as I spoke, walking out the door to Kira's screams directed, specifically at me. She rattled off every name in the book in the exact tone a much-loving sister would talk to you. Instead of driving home, I went to my uncle. From what Kira had told me, I knew where he was, and I knew that I had to act quickly if I was going to try to save his life.

I got to the hospital about an hour later, not knowing at the time that not only had Kira lied to me about where to go but that Jenkins had set up a trap there, one that led me to the police. That night, May 25th, I was detained for what was called the "attempt to release a 'classified patient.'" What made the situation even more confusing, besides that I was in the back of a cop car, was that when I called Kira about an hour later, she acted like she had zero idea that it would happen. As angry as I was at not only Kira but also a detective whom I never trusted, I encouraged a search while being detained; a search that resulted in the confiscation,and investigation, of the device that I discussed earlier. I was released about two hours later after a surprisingly informative interrogation about a case that I knew nearly nothing about. When I got out, all I wanted to do was to call Kira. As much as she was the last person I wanted to talk to, I knew my detainment was scheduled by one of the two individuals I had met with earlier. "Kira, before I kill you and Jenkins, I need you to be honest and tell me if you knew a single thing about what just happened."

Kira spoke in tears. It was the first time I had ever heard her cry, the first time I had ever seen her not run away from one of her family's traumas. "I really didn't know... but Jenkins knows you recorded that, and I'm telling you, don't get into legal stuff with this guy. He has too much power. So please, sis, stay out of it and get out of here."

I was shocked. I didn't know why at the time, but for the first time, I trusted everything she said. "Kira, I already gave them the tape; they said Eli is going to be reexamined before he is given back to whatever Jenkins has going on. I'm going to be fine, though, Kira," I laughed softly at her comments. Jenkins seemed like an extreme loner, not close to someone who would have a bunch of connections with important people, especially when it came to the legal system.

Kira: "Okay, okay, I will try to talk him out of it, but seriously, Nicole, leave. You're going to be someone of interest if anything is revealed in the scans."

I agreed and hung up quickly. After everything that had happened, if she thought for a second that I was going to run like I wasn't innocent about any of this, then my sister knew me less than I thought. I proceeded to drive home, waiting for a call, waiting for anything to give me a chance to put this guy where he belonged: prison. Nothing happened for hours: no text from Kira, no cops at my door, no call, no news on the radio. I had almost lost hope that giving up that device had done anything that would have helped my uncle.

That was, until about nine pm. I was watching TV like any other night, cuddled up with my cat, and waiting for the night to drift off before the channel switched. I was startled by it, not even remotely coming to the thought of what the headline would be.

Famous Author Eli Whitts is Dead – Faced Serious Brain Laceration Trauma as a result of Undisclosed and Classified Experiments...

As soon as the news came up, I sprung up, more filled with rage than anything else. The only thing I had on my mind was revenge.. A couple of sporadic texts would come from my sister over the next hour, but I ignored them as I sped over to Jenkins, wanting to do anything but be friendly to the man who had killed my uncle.

CHAPTER 6
A RENEWED PERSPECTIVE

As I sat back against the hospital wall, more confused than ever, I looked at both Nicole and Kira, waiting to see if the story stopped there.

"Wait, so what happened? Obviously, you didn't kill him, but that doesn't explain why you two aren't speaking—or why you'd want me to go to the person who killed your uncle."

Nicole sighed, leaning forward.

Nicole: "Right. When I went to Jenkins, I was detained again, as if it were all a setup. My uncle was very dead—don't get that part mixed up—but the only thing that happened was me, once again, ending up in the back of a cop car. As for the rest, that's up to the girl you've somehow decided to trust with your life— the same sister who has betrayed me more times than I can count."

Kira rolled her eyes, clearly bristling at Nicole's accusation. She hesitated, then spoke up before I could respond.

Kira: "I'm helping Jesse because I know how dangerous Jenkins is. And as for Nicole—once she was arrested and questioned for a supposed conviction of attempted murder, I stepped in and got them to see her as mentally unstable."

Nicole shot back immediately, her voice sharp and indignant.

Nicole: "That's *so* false. Yes, you helped me avoid jail, but only after the so-called evidence of me wanting to kill Jenkins was on *our phone calls*—which *you* recorded and sent to the *fucking* police."

I sat there in stunned silence, my thoughts racing. I wanted to trust Kira. I wanted Nicole's help. But now I wasn't sure if I was even safe sitting in the same room as the two of them.

I got up, almost ready to walk out the door, but something in the back of my mind stopped me. Deep down, I knew Kira was right. I had already told Jenkins too much to leave him in the dark, and there was no way I could deal with him on my own.

Nicole turned to me, her tone calmer but still firm.

Nicole: "Look, Jesse, right?"

I nodded.

Nicole: "I never answered your question. I advocated for you to go back to Jenkins because, as much as I hate to admit it, he *is* smart. He *does* have experience in these areas. He knew I was right about my uncle and even admitted it in the paper I showed you earlier. So, take his words with a grain of salt all you want, but consider this: most of the things he says are true."

I nodded. Like Nicole had said about Kira, I had no rational reason to trust her, but I did. It was probably due to her experience with the entire situation and the unfairness of her current life, but at that time, my trust, when it came to Jenkins, was almost more in the hands of Nicole than Kira.

After a couple of minutes, Kira and I walked out, heading back to her car again, not saying anything. It wasn't the same as before. Instead of an argument or a disconnect, this was more of a non-talking processing time with everything that had just happened. As we got in her car, however, I spoke up immediately. "We need to go see Will and Amy."

Kira glanced at me and giggled. "Yeah, let's go to the college where people think you killed someone so you can get a quick laugh with your friends at a time we don't really have time on our side."

I looked at Kira and rolled my eyes, knowing she was going to be slightly mad at me as I spoke up. "Yeah, I kind of told Will we were going to meet him at the motel we booked, so it's not really a choice type of thing..."

Kira looked at me and started laughing hysterically as she pulled off to the side of the road. "So, you listened to Nicole's story that didn't exactly explain the reliability of people close to you, and then called your friend so that you can talk to him about what? About your classes, or what?"

I didn't know what to say as she pulled back on the road. I thought she liked Will and Amy. I guess the more I thought about it, the dumber it sounded, but again, it was too late to cancel. As we drove to my motel, I tried to speak a couple of times, but Kira seemed more confused with me than ever before.

Kira: "Look, I get you're scared, and you think Will can provide some new perspective because he's literally insane, but dealing with what you're going through, the worst thing we can do is rope more people into this."

I sat back and looked at Kira. I think she even knew that some conversation was going to happen with Will but that she wanted me to end it before it started. I trusted her, I really did. But the stuff Nicole said was still in my mind, and this was my case, not hers. So if I wanted Will to hear about it, he was going to – end of story.

The rest of the drive to our motel room was awkward, to say the least. It seemed like all rides with Kira were like this nowadays. We would be talking about something, migrating the conversation to this unknown situation, and then turning that into an argument and, hence, disconnecting. It was almost like it was planned; every time I was in the car with her, it was just more awkward and more curious than the time before. As we neared the motel, I turned to Kira. Like at the hospital, I knew that we had to know that our friendship was still intact before a potential time of prolonged disagreement.

"Hey, Kira, I'm going to be honest: I can't get what Nicole said out of my head, and I know you don't want me to talk to Will about everything, but I still don't know if I can trust you fully."

I thought she was going to take offense to this. Honestly, I did. I had betrayed her trust before. But also, if I wasn't going to trust her, I probably wouldn't have told her everything that was going on, and planned to be with her until it got solved. I still didn't know whether Will and Amy saw me as a killer or as the same innocent Harvard sophomore. I figured that Will's texting me signaled that he still viewed me the same way or that he hadn't heard about the class incident, but either way, I wanted to talk to him. As much trust I was putting in Kira, I still hadn't really dealt with her outside a brief period in high school. I could say nearly the opposite about Will and Amy, which is the main reason I trusted them as much as I did. And even if he wasn't really going to help in any way, a laugh wouldn't be the worst thing in the world for my mental fortitude.

Kira: "Yeah, look, I can't do anything about the situation with Nicole, and I understand if it's going to take you a bit to trust me again. I have to say, though, that I still don't think talking to him is a good thing. Now, I will support you through this decision, honestly, because I need to make sure that you're safe until all this is resolved, but that doesn't mean I'm going to allow you to explain everything."

I nodded as I looked at her. If she thought I was going to say anything about what Nicole had told me, she was wrong, not just because Will probably didn't know who Nicole was, but mostly because what I heard was supposed to be safe from even my ears, much less an outside perspective. One thing I had to know as we parked, however, was again the reason she was genuinely helping me.

"Wait, Kira, I know you said you're helping to keep me safe from Jenkins or whatever is going on, but I feel like there's more to that."

Kira sighed and sat back in the passenger seat prior to getting out. "Yeah," she nodded, looking at me with true emotion for maybe the first time since I had run to her that morning a couple of days back. "Yeah, I've done the research, and if we can link Jenkins to some type of problem like this, I think I can get my sister unconvicted and set free. I never told her that, so please never bring it up to her, but yeah, I've been trying to find cases like yours for years to latch onto. It just so happened that the person is someone I know, which is you."

I got out of the car and thought about what she had said. Was she using me? Did she want me to go to Jenkins just for a confession? How much was she still lying about? I didn't want to think about any of these questions and create a bigger mystery with her than the voices, but I really couldn't jump my mind from such questions. There would be time for those to be answered, but not now, not when I still had to deal with the emotions and worry that I was always a minute away from yet another trance.

Kira and I walked into our room. As Kira went to the bathroom, I sat on the bed, quickly stunned at the text I had just received.

Will: Yo bro, we are on the way, but I got some notification about one of the classes you said you're in. That shit doesn't have to do with you. Right?

I sat back on the bed. I didn't know what to respond back with or if I needed to ask Kira about it. I did know, though, that the longer I left it on read, the more suspicion it would create. Knowing this, I simply texted back, saying, "Yea, we can talk about it when you get here."

Luckily, Will seemingly never even read the text, as when he got there shortly after, it seemed as if none of his perspectives had changed. Will and Amy walked in, laughing as normal and seemingly happy, an emotion I hadn't really experienced since that night at the carnival. We exchanged some conversation for a short while before things got serious. I think that helped, as Kira seemed to become calmer about the whole situation, and while it still was up in the air exactly how much she was okay with me saying, I at least felt like some small conversation wouldn't affect her train of thought.

Will: "Okay, but seriously, Jesse, what did you mean by saying yeah when I was asking about what I saw on the news?"

I sat back on the bed, sitting next to Kira and across from Will and Amy, who had quickly gone from a fun and emotional state to a much more solemn and serious tone. I knew this conversation was going to go to this, but for some reason, I had hoped it wouldn't. At the same time, however, if I didn't want to explain everything to one of my best friends, I probably wouldn't have been missing from school for days on end and texting him to meet up.

I looked at Kira first, and as soon as I saw her nod, I started to talk. "It was 9 am, normal class, I actually felt good..." The next 20 minutes, I went to almost every detail in that small motel room. I even included minute details that I hadn't shared everything with Kira about that morning. There were small but important details I had kept to myself, such as the state of my classroom accomplices, the stress of the day, and the fact that the teacher had just returned from a two-week absence due to a death in his family.

As good as it felt to get such a weight off my chest, the emotional and facial reactions of two of my best friends—hearing that I was basically a perceived murderer—were something I never thought I'd have to experience.

Not only did they not leave, but Will and Amy seemed more attentive during that long tribulation than I had ever seen them. Will, in particular, stood out. He had been the first one to call such spirits demonic and insane when I mentioned them back on October 12th.

Will: "Wow, I didn't ever perceive you as a murderer, and obviously I still don't, but honestly, like, I really don't know whether to believe you. I mean, the only reason I haven't left is because of how genuine you seem about it. It's almost like you're not lying about everything since that night."

Amy: "Yeah, Uhm, I mean, I'm kind of scared as your friend through all this, and I know Kira has talked about this stuff before, but when she told me you were fine that night, it seems like you obviously weren't. So, are you just not like going back to school?"

I sat back, looking at them and Kira, figuring out the correct but truthful words to say. The last thing I wanted to do was rush my thoughts or, even worse, lie to them, so I decided to sit and think for a couple of seconds. "Yeah, I can't really go back to school. I still don't know if I can even get my things without some type of raid. And yeah, I'm telling the truth, Will. I know it seems near impossible to comprehend, and honestly, I haven't even fully grasped the gravity of all this, but I know what I'm dealing with is real, and I'm scared, so I must figure out why."

Kira looked at me with a concerned look in her eyes as her hand reached over to mine. It was clear she resonated with everything I was feeling.

Kira: "Look, guys, both of you. I honestly didn't want him to talk to you two about it. Jesse thought you would have a different and unique perspective on what we should do to help him, which is the ONLY reason that I'm okay with this whole thing."

Will looked confused at Kira's words, but I nodded, trying to signal to Will that I trusted her fully. The conversation went on for a bit longer. We discussed thoughts such as what I was to do next, how Will could get my stuff for me, and how I was even going to figure out what was going on. I could tell Kira was getting more comfortable with everything that was going on, but she still seemed confused by everything. I decided to figure out why as I turned to her.

"Kira, what's going on? You haven't said anything since they got here."

Kira looked at me and then turned her crystal eyes into a deep stare aimed at Will. "I'm just confused, Jess; you thought he would have some insight, and all I have heard is the same ideas Jenkins or I could have told you to do. So, Will? Any ideas of what's going on?"

Will: "Well, yeah." My uncle's name is Titan. He is huge into some transcendental stuff like this, and from what he has told me, these types of things are normal when experiencing such an out-of-body experience. I would say he most likely has another episode, this time being a much more personal version when it comes to the fears he really possesses. Nah, but honestly, I would just say to stay out of the way. I don't know who you have helping him, but it's a process you must be super careful because, based on what he said, it's going to get worse before it gets better."

I was more confused than ever at that moment. Amy looked just as confused as me, almost like she had never met the guy who had just spoken.

The only one who wasn't surprised but instead looked almost offended was Kira, who got up before scrolling on her phone in a hurried way and calling out to Will, saying, "Can we go outside and talk, just briefly."

Will nodded, and before I knew it, I was inside that dark motel room with Amy. We didn't talk and sat in silence as Will and Kira had some "mysterious" conversation about some supposed uncle that had struck a nerve in Kira. I glanced at Amy, asking her if she knew or had met this Titan.

Amy: "I mean, yeah, once, but he was super quiet and reserved. He definitely didn't seem to know anything so cruel or mysterious."

I nodded as I laid back on the hard mattress. I had no idea what they were talking about. All I knew was that it was about Titan, about me, about some type of secretive path to this whole thing that, again, Kira knew about and wasn't going to disclose to me. Looking back on it, however, I was happy I didn't know what they were discussing, such as Uncle Jenkins and anything else Kira hid from me, which proved to be the right decision.

Kira: "You didn't tell me he was your fucking uncle," she said as she slammed the door behind her. "I heard about him through Colin, but I never connected you to it."

Will: "What does it matter, Kira? I haven't spoken to him in years, and just because Colin and Titan were a part of your dead uncle's case because of Nicole, it doesn't mean he is connected to this."

Kira sighed. It was like she didn't know whether to be mad or happy.

Will: "Either way, though, if you knew I knew this much, then why did you keep telling Jesse not to talk to me about what's going on in his life? We both know I can help."

Kira: "Because Jesse is already so stressed with stuff what he doesn't know? Because the last time I trusted you during an actual episode of his, you laughed at his descriptions? Because I didn't know that your uncle was a contributor to my uncle's death? Like why you think, Will, pick a reason."

Will sighed as he sat on the hood of his truck. "To be fair, Kira, I didn't think it would matter that much if I brought my uncle up, especially since Jesse doesn't know the guy. Thanks to you, though, he's probably super nervous and suspicious now about anything having to do with him."

Kira: "Fine, Will," she sighed, "Maybe I screwed up this, but again, if I knew who you were or more like who your uncle was, I probably would've just met with you. Instead this whole thing has Jesse more nervous than anything!... Let's just go back inside. I got my anger and confusion out. Now again, we need to make sure we keep Jesse sane."

As I sat inside patiently waiting for them to come back, I again wondered if they would even tell me what their conversation was about. My guess was that nothing would be said in Amy's presence, and I would be given an outline once I was alone with Kira, but again, I honestly had no idea. I didn't know how vital their conversation was; I didn't know why Kira seemed so amped about it.

Just as these thoughts circled my brain, they both walked in, sitting across from each other like nothing had happened. My immediate reaction was to ask questions, but when I started to speak and saw Kira signal not to, I stayed quiet. The conversation did begin again, but it didn't last more than 5 minutes. Kira and Will seemed to be careful in their words before Will got up, whispered something to Amy, and left. Will, my best friend, had left without saying anything, not even a goodbye or good luck. I would have been more worried about trusting him, but since Kira seemed to, it made sense to do so.

I waited about 10 minutes after they left before I decided to bring up the "secretive" discussion that was taking place. "Kira, what was happening out there? It seems like this Titan guy struck a nerve, but I have no idea who he is. Will has never even mentioned an uncle."

Kira looked at me before getting up; she ended up sending a couple of texts while she paced around the room, seemingly having her mind complete of different ways to deal with the situation. Again, it was a situation, my mind and voices that I was hearing, and out of seemingly the two people that I knew the best, I was in the dark the most.

Usually, something like this wouldn't phase me. In almost any situation where I had a problem, I would always be willing to listen to some other perspective when it came to an expert, but this was different. Not just because they were my age and some of my best friends but more because I didn't think there was such a thing as an expert on this topic. And considering the "expert" was a detective who seemed to mess up and criminalize more than find solutions, my idea of no expert being in play seemed reliable.

Kira: "It's hard to explain, Jesse," she said as she glanced up at me from her phone. "Jenkins just told me he found something, though, so we should get going."

I was so flustered by the conversation outside that, at that moment, I completely ignored the fact that Jenkins had given me hope of finding the solution. I immediately stopped Kira before she got up, filled with annoyance and a form of rage toward her for maybe the first time since high school. "Kira, stop. Obviously, the Titan thing struck a nerve, and I need to know why. You can't just keep involving new people in my case without including the person who is experiencing this. Like, I get your sister is in an asylum, and Jenkins did all that to your uncle, but that doesn't mean that you have any idea at all what I'm going through. This isn't just like some kick in the back every once in a while. It's an unwavering fear that every day could be my last normal one, that any day I could indirectly hurt another human because it appears I have zero control of myself. The simple idea that if I don't find what's happening, my life could be over is a terrifying thought."

Kira looked at me with solemn concern. I don't think she knew how much pain I was embracing, and honestly, I didn't either. Whether we both wanted to admit it or not, the situation was entirely new for both of us. This wasn't just some medical thing that was skewed. This was a full-blown demonic phase that most people would commit suicide to stop it. I didn't even know if the screams were telling me anything, I didn't know if those children I had heard that night were real, and I didn't even know why Will knew so much, but Kira had to know how I really felt, it was the only way we were going to start making progress.

Kira: "Yeah, uhm. Look, Titan was a friend of Jenkins who was a part of that whole digging my uncle up thing. Jenkins was never good at being truly secretive when it came to the outside world, so he called Titan, Will's uncle, to help him because Titan was a known culprit on what we call the dark web. He seemed a normal guy the one time I talked to him, but I never trusted him. So, I spied on all of Jenkins and Titan's conversations. During those times, I found out why he was so well known, and when Will brought him up, I freaked out because I hadn't heard that name in almost three years."

I sighed, sitting back. Maybe she was lying; I had no idea, but she seemed to be truthful, and I had no other choice but to trust her. "What did you find out, though, like in those conversations you were talking about."

Kira looked at me clearly, not wanting to say anything she was about to say. "It's complicated, Jesse. I promise I will tell you after this is all over, but if I tell you, and he happens to be a single part of all this, then it will just make you worry more."

I got up after she spoke, finally acknowledging her past words about Jenkins having a clue. Kira and I walked out of the room, walked back to her car, and drove over to Jenkins. For the first time in a while, this ride wasn't as awkward. It's not like much was said, but we seem to be on the same page in terms of a lot of things now. I knew I had to trust her around Jenkins to stay safe, and most importantly, I knew she would tell me anything I needed to know about my case without worrying me. The drive was a quick one and one of the few times that week I got some decent sleep. I hadn't slept much since that first night, but now, for the first time, I felt somewhat at peace when it came to my emotions.

Neither Kira nor I had any idea what Jenkins was going to say; we just hoped it would be necessary, and I just wished I had gotten past most of the unknown and would start to check off the questions I had as opposed to creating new ones.

CHAPTER 7
A CLUE AFTER ALL

When we finally arrived at Jenkins's, the worn-out house seemed much more normal. Instead of having no idea who this guy was, I now knew more than I even probably wanted to. Not that I had any definite opinion of him or even trusted him, but at least I wasn't walking into a black hole like the first time. Kira and I walked up to his door, rang the doorbell, and waited for the mysterious detective to confront us.

I found myself surprisingly calm at that moment. Not just because I knew Jenkins, like I said before, but because I felt like there was an actual purpose to being here. The first time wasn't even my decision, but instead, it was an impulse decision by Kira, as opposed to now, a meeting that concerned me and hopefully would answer more than one question.

Jenkins opened the door, looking at both of us with a slight smile on his face. "Thanks for coming so quickly," he said as he let us in. "We have a lot to talk about."

I walked in, immediately noticing the cleanness of the place. The first time I had been here, the floors and walls were ravaged with dust, almost like someone hadn't lived there in months, but now, the place was damn near spotless.

Kira and I sat down next to each other on the wool couch that faced the main dining room. Kira almost looked as worried as I about whatever Jenkins was about to say. "Okay, so what do you have for us? Anything to provide me any context about who is doing this?" These words came out of my mouth in a sort of rumbled tone, one that came from my fear and worry about the result of such conversation.

Jenkins: "Yeah, well, kind of. I figured out how it's being transmitted to you and sort of why you are experiencing such phases..."

I looked at Kira, more confused than ever. So, had he figured out anything to actually help me? Was this just another lie like the ones he spewed to Nicole? Trying to figure out exactly what he found out, I asked him, saying, "So tell me then, Detective, are you saying I did something to somehow attract me to it?"

Jenkins: "Kind of. Okay, as far as the transmission, it seems to be some interface that is connected to your inner brainwaves. Not like Eli, but more crucially important. It's almost like some inner headphone that has been demented or gained access, so you feel the full effect of all the voices you hear."

I really thought my questions were going to be answered, and now I sat there, more confused than before. A hearing interface? Not only had I never even heard of such a thing, but it seemed so out-of-body that it bordered on impossible. But again, so did this whole situation, the death of my teacher, all of it.

Jenkins: "As far as why you were targeted, I have spent most of my time trying to figure this out. The only thing I can think of is that you hurt or disrupted some rational thought, some thought that traced an emotion to a being or someone with access to such advanced tech. I'm sorry, Jesse, the idea that I am right about seems so out of thought. It's crazy, even for myself, but any other rational explanation has led to a dead end. I want to help, I really do, but your case doesn't make sense with the stuff you've told me."

I didn't do anything. I didn't sigh, didn't lay back, none of it. I just sat there, stunned at what he had said. Did I think he was crazy? Well, yeah, of course, I did, but that didn't mean that what he was saying was untrue. It made me believe him more to say what he said than if he had started spewing some random information about brain function or about me being sick. Jenkins almost seemed to know too much, and it was like he had predicted everything to happen as if he knew how such an interface that he mentioned was working. "So, how did you figure that out? Maybe you can't share all the stuff you do behind the scenes, but how did you come up with an interface description? I have ideas about all this, and even my friend had some, even bringing up some reoccurrence that his uncle predicted."

As soon as I said this, Jenkins stopped smiling. His smile turned to a cold and serious stare; one pointed directly at my inner brain. It was so weird. I didn't say the guy's name, and I didn't even mention Will as my friend, but as if Kira had reacted back at the hotel, he seemed stunned. Kira looked at me, making me even more confused. She was just as baffled as me. "Sorry sir, are you ok?"

The detective nodded. As good or bad of a detective as he was, he knew how to lie, how to deceive, and most importantly, how to hide the emotions that seemed to eat him inside.

Jenkins: "Yeah, I'm fine. The reason I know so much about what may be changing your emotions is due to my past. I'm sure you know about it, but I experienced a situation very similar to yours. I never completely figured it out because of my young age. But, the man who helped me, made me want to do the same thing, mostly so I could prove him wrong and to find out what was really going on. But before I go on, who was this uncle?"

I glanced at Kira, waiting for her reaction to a topic that I thought would be an emotional one if I went on to expand on it. Kira shrugged, looking at me to signal that it was my choice what I explained. "Yeah, the uncle is named Titan. I've personally only met him once, so I don't know much about him, but my friend seemed pretty genuine in his trust for the man."

I thought this would freeze Jenkins once again, but nearly the opposite happened. Jenkins got up, walked over to his desk, pulled out a piece of paper, and walked back, handing the piece of paper to Kira. I sat back as Kira turned the paper from my eyes and examined it. Obviously, I didn't know what was on it, but seeing her face light up in shock told me enough. "What was on that paper, sir?" I said, turning to Jenkins.

Jenkins: "Titan Black's dark web profile report. He's currently one of the most wanted people in the world due to his complications in cases such as mine and yours, and he can't be found. Basically, I don't know how your friend even got a hold of his uncle, but he's not the person that you wanted to hear your story."

As he finished, Kira handed me the paper, a half-ripped one at that, a printed FBI report on an uncle that seemed dull and off-putting the one time I'd met him. As I glanced at it, the only thing I wanted to do was call Will and yell at him for what he did, but I knew that would only make things worse. Now, did I think Titan had anything to do with my case? No, but I did think he had some odd relationship with Jenkins, making him somewhat untrustworthy.

POLICE REPORT (May 12th – 1993)

TITAN BLACK - #199643

Titan Black - wanted for committing unsanctioned, and possibly, illegal experiments and activities which may have involved dark magic. He has been known to perform such acts, along with other manipulations, on Colin Jenkins and the now deceased, Eli Whitts. Black has been missing for two weeks. He has been known to access unauthorized websites concerning disturbing activities such as gravedigging and other dark arts. Black was known as a former colleague and friend of Colin Jenkins, a very intelligent but skewed man.

As I read it, I didn't know what to think. It was so obvious he could help, and I think he did, mostly through his warning to Will that another event would happen. And for the first time in my life, most likely due to my slight insanity, I cried to myself, hoping for such an episode to occur. I don't know why. I just figured that if Jenkins had actually seen what happened, then he would be able to solve it or at least give me a better clue than a supposed interface. The only words I could mutter out, however, were, "So what part does he play, and what do I do now? Am I going to have another trance?" I was so lost in my words that when I sat back next to Kira, it felt like my heart was skipping multiple beats in between each trace. Every second that passed while Jenkins thought felt like an eternity. Before he could speak to respond, however, the sound of his ringing house phone took me by storm. *Rrrring Rrrring Rrrrrring.*

It was no different from the sound I had heard a thousand times prior, except that it was. I wasn't hearing anything abnormal but was only mentally alarmed by the three rings as Jenkins went to pick it up.

Jenkins: "Mhm, got it. So, is it 20 minutes? Sounds good, sir, thanks."

I looked up at him, wondering what the call was, as he hung up the phone. What was happening in 20 minutes? Did it involve me? I wanted to find out, and wouldn't have to wait long.

Jenkins: "Kira, your appointment was approved. You should have around an hour with the corpse."

"Wait... corpse? Kira, what is Jenkins talking about? Whose body are you planning on seeing?"

Kira looked at me as she laughed softly, "I thought it would be obvious. I didn't mean to scare you."

Jenkins: "Yeah, Kira told me about how much you doubted what had happened with Eli Whitts, so we both decided it would be okay for you to see what was really going on with him, honestly, if nothing else, to show you what the worst possible outcome would be with your situation: Death."

As I got with Kira, about to leave, I looked back at Jenkins. Maybe he had forgotten about it, but I hadn't. My question, my wondering about the case of Mr. Black and why he was even involved, was still up in the air. "Before we go, and thanks for your help, but does that uncle of Will's actually matter at all?"

Jenkins: "For your case, probably not. For the result of my case, yeah, he does. Look, I told you to be careful, and that's the main advice I would give you, but when you see this body. Both of you. It's a hard thing to look at and examine, and I would recommend you take a glance, get an update on any existing wave activity, and leave. I don't think there's anything super important you're going to find, and even if you did, the trauma wouldn't be worth it."

Kira and I walked out and went to her car. All I wanted was for this to be over, for me to be able to go back to college. It was so weird. When I had a boring life in college, I always wanted to be active and known, and now that I was, all I wanted was to be boring and alone. It was a classic sense of the old saying, "Be careful what you wish for," but instead in a dragged-out and chronic version. As we drove to the hospital, Kira and I only spoke briefly. Of course, there were a million things I wanted to ask her, but again, I could never find the right time. Every time I was about to speak up, something would happen. Every time I thought I found an answer, another question would arise. It was a constant cycle of disappointment and mistrust that kept leading me down a rabbit hole that was only getting bigger.

Once we got to the hospital, we got out, still not saying much except the words we needed to due to access. It wasn't because we weren't on the same page or didn't like each other, but honestly, the opposite. It seemed like, at that moment, Kira and I both understood the emotional toll the situation would take on us if anything wrong happened. Kira was about to see her uncle's body for the first time in 3 years, and the last time I was about to do was cause an argument.

Doctor: "Hey, it's good to see both of you. You guys will have an hour. There will be supervision, however.

Not voice monitors, so anything you say is free, but just for security. I trust both of you will be respectful of human decomposition, though?"

We nodded and walked towards the autopsy room to find his body covered with a light blue cloth. The room smelled of dead carcasses, probably the most preposterous smell of my life. As much as I wanted to run out of the room surrounded by dead-smelling bodies, I knew Kira, for some reason, wanted to see him. As the doctor closed the door behind us, I looked at Kira, saying, "Now, can you tell me why we are here? I get it's your uncle, and you didn't believe the whole brainwave thing, but that was years ago, and he's now been unburied three times."

Kira nodded as she lifted the cloth, uncovering Eli's deceased face. I looked at it with shock. Not only was his face a stern pale white, but the nerves laid on his deceased skull, almost like they still had life. There weren't muscles; there wasn't even much skin, but still veins, popping out from the man's outer brain like he had never died in the first place. I wanted to start asking questions, maybe even see if the doctors knew anything, but this case was closed, and the man was dead. There wasn't much I could do. As I started to look at his body and the discoloration on the skin, Kira spoke up.

Kira: "I wanted to show you that Jenkins wasn't totally wrong about my uncle. Those veins we see, they shouldn't be there. The doctors' report never even says anything about them, and obviously, there is some type of abnormality. I just can't figure it out. And most of all, I wanted to come here to get our mind off the uncle of your friend because, honestly, it probably has nothing to do with you. We need to have a clear mind Jesse, and the idea that your friend's relative was the one possibly infecting your mind just seemed dumb."

I nodded in agreement as I continued to glance at the body, unsure of what to believe about the last hour at Jenkins'. Looking back, it felt like Jenkins was implying that someone had essentially "connected a Bluetooth device" inside me, taking control of my sensations.

Yeah, that made no logical sense.

But then again, was this even the time to think in logical terms? If there was ever a moment to accept that the most insane explanation might actually be the truth, this was it.

As Kira meticulously examined the body, I walked out of the room and headed toward the doctors, hoping to find some medical explanation.

Doctor: "The disease Mr. Whitts had lined up with the original nerve damage 100 percent. But all this stuff about the nerves enlarging or even pulsing to a heart rate three years after death? Yeah, that's almost unheard of.

"The only possible explanation I could think of is intermittent exposure to light and sensors. But that's something you almost never see once a body is buried."

I thanked her and returned to the autopsy room, finding Kira still intently focused on the body.

"Hey, Kira," I said softly. "I get why we came, but I'm fine. If you're not finding anything, maybe we should just go."

Kira stood up slowly, casting one last glance at the body before walking over to me.

"Yeah, uh… we can go. I was just trying to figure out what to do with him. At this point, I don't even know if burying him is the right thing to do—not after all the disrespect that's been done to his body."

Her voice trembled slightly, the emotion in her words unmistakable.

Considering neither Kira nor Nicole had ever mentioned their parents, I had a strong feeling that Eli played a significant role in their upbringing. I wasn't about to ask, though—not out of fear, but out of respect.

Still, the mystery of who Eli truly was in their lives lingered in my mind. If Nicole hadn't mentioned him during her story, I'd have no real idea of his significance. Not that it mattered—at least, not right now.

I decided it was best for me to leave Kira alone for a bit, so while she continued to examine and look around the edges of her dead uncle, I walked outside to her car, got in, and jumped on my phone. Through all that had happened in the past day, I had forgotten about the conversation that I had with Will, so when he texted me talking about my stuff, I was surprised.

Will: "I went to get your stuff, but I couldn't. The owner of the building wouldn't let me have the key to your room and just kept asking me these weird questions about you. I'm not saying that you're a known convict to half the school, but I am saying that if you need to get your stuff, to be super careful."

I looked at the text and spent the remaining ten minutes I had alone. trying to contemplate how I was going to tell and, more importantly, convince Kira to help me. Maybe I was overreacting, and the school never even thought I had anything to do with the death. Either way, I knew I had to be in and out of that campus perimeter.

Kira walked out of the car a bit later, getting in and not saying anything. Inside, I knew asking a risky question at the time wasn't a smart idea, but I also didn't really have time to waste. "Kira, we need to go back to my apartment. I have stuff there I need to get, and Will wasn't allowed in."

Surprisingly enough to me, Kira agreed, not saying anything besides a quick nod of acknowledgment as she started to drive. Looking back on it, she probably only did such to prevent an argument in which she simply didn't have the energy to participate. "So, what's going to happen to Eli?" I wanted to ask her about it, but finding the right things to say was always different, so I figured the shorter the response, the better.

Kira: "Uhm, I'm getting him cremated. It's not going to happen for a while, but that's what I figured out was the best course of action. I mean, Nicole might kill me for it, but, uh, I'm sure she will understand eventually. I hope…"

I honestly agreed with her, but to not get her sister on board seemed so weird. I get she was in an institution, but Kira still could've called. Nicole seemed normal when I met her, but she also seemed like a person I wouldn't want to piss off. "Why didn't you run it by her?"

Kira: "Cause," she said as a tear rolled down the side of her cheek, "I didn't have the energy to argue with Nicole about what the best course of action would've been. I knew she would disagree with the whole cremation thing, so I just made the decision and signed the paperwork myself."

I nodded as we drove to my apartment. As we got closer to my school, however, I started to feel a shivering cold breeze across my chest. It wasn't from the AC. The windows weren't down; it was simply a cold and bitter feeling that raced across my heart. I thought to myself at that moment that going back to my school, to anywhere near my school, was a good idea. I was stunned in my heart multiple times in the next couple of minutes, and as Kira pulled up to the building, my eyes closed, unable to be opened, but still giving me the ability to see trances through the darkness.

CHAPTER 8
ON THE RUN

Due to a shake on my shoulder, I immediately woke up, only seeing Kira's worried face in my peripheral view.

"What was that?" she said as she opened her car door.

The worried look on her face confused me; I knew this wasn't the 3rd episode that Will mentioned as it wasn't personal, wasn't for long, and couldn't even be heard. "I have no idea. It's probably stress, so let's just get it over with." I couldn't tell her what happened because I didn't know. Like I said, I was almost 100% sure this wasn't what was affecting me, but at the same time, I never felt like I was different at all during all that. My vision didn't stop, my emotions weren't halted, nothing.

I started to get out of the car, but Kira stopped me. "Jesse, let me go in and get it. Just give me the key. You stay in the car in case something goes wrong."

I nodded. I didn't know if she would be able to get my stuff, but I gave her my key, moving to the driver's seat and hoping whatever she thought could go wrong wouldn't happen. As I waited, trying to be as patient as possible, my head turned from side to side, looking for anything I would consider hazardous. A couple of minutes went by after Kira left before an email alert popped up on my phone. In short words, the email was a statement about the death of the Harvard professor and pinned me as the culprit. It stated I was a possible suspect in the case, showing a portrait of my face and asking for any information about my whereabouts. Fearful was a slim word for the emotion that was overtaking me at that moment. I immediately got out of the car, locked it, and ran inside trying to notify Kira. As I ran through the thinned-out hallways, I saw people taking second looks at me. The more people I saw, the more stress overtook me. I started to realize that as opposed to just wanting to find who was causing all this, now I now had to prevent a life in prison. Even if I did find the guy, I didn't know if it would prevent it from whatever evidence they had, but I knew that was my only shot. As I got to the hallway where my living area was, I saw Kira running towards me carrying a small bag of my stuff.

Kira: "Jesse, what the hell are you doing in here? We got to go, like now."

She seemed more stressed than I was—maybe even mad at me—but that made sense. Kira and I sprinted down the hall, pushing past one or two people who thought they could "catch" me. As we burst outside, the sirens grew louder, each second bringing the authorities closer.

We jumped into her car and sped off without saying a word. Relief washed over me, but it was fleeting. I didn't think they had any real evidence of me doing anything—besides being insane—but the last thing Kira and I wanted was to stick around and find out.

At this point, it wasn't even about her caring for me. She knew I was the only way to get to whoever—or whatever—was behind these trances. I also knew Will was right about some kind of third vision. I just didn't know how it would happen or where it would lead us.

Kira drove for about an hour, past the motel we'd been staying in and into the countryside. We avoided populated areas; even though I wasn't considered dangerous by the authorities, a murderer was a murderer.

To the public eye—and to anyone who didn't know the situation—I had killed someone. I had killed my teacher in cold blood, with no visible remorse.

As we drove, I wondered if I should've stayed instead of running and pretended to be as shocked as everyone else when it happened. But it was too late for regrets.

The best thing I could do now was stay with Kira and find somewhere safe to regroup.

Eventually, we arrived at a small ranch nestled in a vast grass field, surrounded only by yellowing grass and grazing animals. For the first time in a while, I felt a faint sense of security.

"So, where can we go?" I asked as Kira parked her car.

Kira sighed, her tone reflective.

Kira: "It's complicated, Jesse. Here is obviously safe—it's my property and far from everything. Other than that... I mean, Jenkins' place is probably safe. He won't aligns with the police. Maybe the asylum, too, since we've already been there. I told them everything, and they didn't seem to care then, so I doubt they will now."

I stepped out of the car, confused, and turned to her.

"What exactly did you tell them? Just because they didn't care *then* doesn't mean they'll believe you if we have to go back. Worse than that, how do I know they aren't already looking for me because of the parts of your story they *did* believe?"

Kira: "Just forget about it Jesse."

The house, if you want to call it that, was seemingly made from old and worn-down wood planks that were warped. It was held up by some rusted metal poles and seemed to be only standing for the point of being used as a last resort. The inside was fair, with a bedroom, couch, small old-time TV, and a kitchen stocked with what people today would consider survival food. It was almost perfect for everything we were going through: out of the way, peaceful, and away from any difficulties that a normal society would create.

The next week went by in a surprisingly dull manner. Kira and I would wake up and go about our day. She would normally leave to do whatever she needed to do while I stayed back in my thoughts. While some might consider this life boring, it was customary for me. Like I said, I spent a lot of time in my apartment thinking, so now being able to do it with the light of the sunrise beating across my eyes was honestly an improvement. I never asked Kira where she was going, mostly because I knew that she would tell me anything I needed to know. That week was one that grew the trust between Kira and me significantly. We were alone. Besides the people she might be speaking with or working with when she left, I was all she had, and for me, besides a couple of texts, she was the only one I ever talked to. Now, saying this, Kira and I didn't really talk much. We seemed to almost be on the same page every time one of us needed something, but most conversations were short-lived. We weren't living together because we were soulmates; we lived in this shack due to the safety it provided. Our relationship had gone from something of her care for me to a more mutual agreement to work together. While it was not what I had envisioned when Amy first brought up the idea of a date, it was what I needed at that moment.

It was October 30th, the day before Halloween, a holiday that I used to strive for as a kid, but now was just another reason to worry. Not that I believed in superstitions, ghosts, or anything of the matter, but if whatever was making these trances was trying to mess with me, the coincidence of Halloween would make too much sense. That day was the first day that Will had texted me more than once. While he kept reminding me that he was still there for me, I started to feel like he was trying to distance himself from the situation. During our conversation that day, I asked him why he even knew so much about my situation, to which he simply responded saying, "I told you, my uncle." I was honestly annoyed with Will at that moment. Was it because I was getting lazy and tired of seemingly finding zero progress on my case? Probably both, but at that moment, I only felt disappointed. And considering he texted me to call him later that night, I kind of figured out that my annoyance was shown in the way I spoke. I waited to call him until Kira got back.. As far as I was concerned, he didn't know where we were, so I needed to make sure she was on board with me calling him about his uncle.

When I asked, Kira stopped, nodding to me and saying, "Go ahead, but I'm not going to be in this conversation. His uncle is a sensitive topic for me, so I think it's best for whatever he tells you to be between the both of you. Just tell me if anything impactful is said."

I nodded. At that moment, I guess I had forgotten about the whole thing of them talking privately outside earlier, and then, the entire police report on Will's uncle.. Every time something about him had come up, it seemed to be necessary. I never knew why, though, which was why I was going to call Will that night. However, the first thing Will asked was surprising to me at that moment.

Will: "Hey Jesse, first off, where are you? Your friends from Harvard are spamming me. And even weirder, your mom called me. Like, I get you're in question with the whole teacher thing, but you can't just hide yourself."

I thought I was a hundred percent ready for that conversation before those words he spoke. My mom had texted him. I hadn't spoken to my mom in years. Ever since I entered college, I kind of let her and her addiction ravel out of my existence. It was one of the reasons I was so quiet. I used to love my mom. She raised my sister and me without any help, without any father, or worse, a father who showed up once a year with the reason to "not feel like a bad father." In that moment, I had gone from being focused and interested in my uncle's life to a state of guilt and self-punishment for the pain that I had somehow lost my mom. I didn't know if she had heard about what happened and decided it would somehow be a convenient time to check on me or if she was worried about me for the first time since I was 16. She was the main reason it was so hard for me to trust anyone, and now that I did with Kira and Will, she was trying to reenter my life like nothing had happened. The reason I was in Harvard in the first place was because of her anyway. A gift in her mind that was an infection to any hope of the fun socializing life I had dreamed about in high school. My whole life up to my college experience was based on impressing her. A woman who was so strict on her kids and so on edge, she fell into an addiction of a variety of relaxation methods. "Oh, uhm. OK, I'll call her after. But I can't tell you where Kira and I are. The last thing I want to do is endanger you or Kira."

I couldn't see Will's face at that moment, but by the tone of his next words, I would describe him as surprised.

Will: "Look, if I was remotely scared, do you really think I would be talking to you? But anyway, what did you want to talk about? Your spamming earlier kind of indicated something was stressing you out."

"Yeah. Every time I hear your uncle brought up, someone around me gets super personal about it. Jenkins, you, Kira. Everyone I know knows this guy but won't explain to me why he is so bad. And if you and Kira are right that he had nothing to do with my case, then again, why does it matter who he was."

Will: "Okay, Jesse, slow down. My uncle was a bad guy; he went missing, and yes, it's almost impossible that he knows anything about your case. The last time I tried to contact him was after your motel, and he left it "unread". Kira and I thought the guy was dead, but he's not. The guy is on the most wanted list for his knowledge, and you're worried about a charge you didn't even commit."

I nodded to myself at that moment and explained to the best of my ability where Kira and I were. Kira, of course, knew I was saying this and seemed okay with it, so I didn't regret it. "Okay, now that you know that, why did you know so much about it, about why my case was going the way it was, and about the third trance I'm supposed to hear."

Will: "That's more complicated. Look, I was lucky enough to have two parents who truly let me do whatever I wanted, but there was a blockage from some freedoms, which was my Uncle Titan. He was always a man who saw the worst in everything, so in short. When Jenkins first experienced his sensations years ago, my uncle was right there to assist him."

He wasn't there for Jenkins' sake; however, it was more for his own. Now, while he did figure out what was wrong with Jenkins when he told him, Jenkins thought he was insane and pushed him out of his life. That was probably the most challenging time in his life. My uncle went into a dark place, knowing he could have saved Jenkins from the life that my uncle is scared to live right now.

I sat back on the couch, my breathing increasing in pace. "Wait, so what was the issue with Jenkins and..." I sighed as I spoke my next words, not knowing if I should tell him everything, even though deep inside, I knew I was going to either way. "I saw a police report that also included Kira's uncle. Did he tell you about that?"

Will stopped for a second. It was almost like he had never even seen the report I was referencing. "Yeah, my uncle heard about Mr. Whitts seeing Jenkins,. But, then he kind of disappeared from my life for a while. He told me afterward that his goal was to find the cause of Eli's death before Jenkins, in the hope that Jenkins would feel a disappointment great enough to stop his madness. Obviously, he failed, which resulted in a statement Kira's uncle was paid to give before his death that basically included Titan as the reason for his sudden death."

Will stopped in his words. Unlike Kira, who I thought was pausing to formulate a lie, Will seemed to be trying to find the truth in the rush of emotions that crossed his mind.

Will: "That was the last time I talked to him." His voice got solemn as he continued to speak. "I know about your case because I texted him about what I saw that night at the theme park, so all I was doing was basically telling you word for word what he told me. And as far as Jenkins, my uncle basically concluded that he was a genius, a very screwed up one at that, but at the end of the day, a genius. When it came to Eli, he never really gave me an answer. I know he's just as much on the run as you, except he really doesn't seem to communicate with anyone."

I listened to him carefully, making sure that if I responded, my response would be one of honesty and one that was genuine.

Will and I continued to discuss any next steps we wanted to take and whether it was a good idea for the two of us to continue to communicate. And while I knew it was keeping me sane to be able to talk to someone other than Kira, it became clear to me that it would be best for us not to speak as much.

The next couple of hours after we hung up were spent in thought. I had become accustomed to being able to think about the most random things in these moments, ideas that would be considered genuinely crazy by anyone I would have shared them with. Think of the craziest idea you can think of, and it had probably crossed my mind. After about two hours, the only thing that had become clear to me was that I had to have some type of conversation with my mom. I knew it was going to be awkward and most likely wouldn't change a single thing about our relationship, but I knew it had to happen. I opened my phone and scrolled down until I saw her number at the bottom of a long list of names – Natalie Owens.

Ring... Ring... Each time I felt my phone buzz, I had less and less hope that anyone was on the other line. A part of me was hoping she had forgotten about me, that the lady who called Will had the wrong number. As a matter of fact, Will had never told me what she had told him besides she was worried. I wasn't even sure that he talked to her. Should I have been more thankful to her after all the struggles she had? Maybe, but I almost lost any leeway for forgiveness I had for her when I was sixteen.

The day after my sister left for college, the house was already missing her upbeat emotion. I spent a lot of the time in those twenty-four hours thinking about how to live now that she was gone. I don't think my sister ever realized it until I talked to her about four months back, but she was the only reason my mom and I dealt with each other. Every time she helped me, she made me hope that my selfish dad was still in the picture more and more. My mom came into my room, clearly not on this planet when it came to her senses and started to rant about the disappointment I had been to her all those years. Even though I knew she was under the influence, I didn't care. To be honest, the fact that she was so high only made every word pierce what little sympathy I had for her even more. The ranting went on for about twenty minutes before it stopped when fainted from whatever she was on at the time. There I was, a sixteen-year-old kid in northern Massachusetts, a kid who was already lost in life as he sat on his bed and only saw his mom face down on the tile in front of him.

When I said that I went to Harvard because of my mom, it wasn't because of her motivation, her passion, or even the fact that she had gone there as a graduate. It was more the envy I had against her, the hate that I had for her, and the desire to do anything possible to prove her wrong. The only reason I ever even got into Harvard was because of my essay. My GPA was average at best. My test scores were under par. The essay was written in pure hate, in pure regret for living under a mother who was so mad at herself with her husband leaving that she took it out on the one person who slightly reminded her of him. The last sentence of my essay said, "We won't talk for years, that's okay. I couldn't ever forgive you for the hate, the agony, the treacherous drama I've had to endure. But I will struggle with the forgiveness between us forever..."

And as my mother picked up, the last sentence of the essay reigned and replayed in my mind: A path to forgiveness is a struggle for a life so scary.

CHAPTER 9
THE STRUGGLE OF FREEDOM

Mom: "Jesse? Is that really you? How are you doing? I heard everything. What's going on?"

For whatever reason, the last thing I wanted to believe was that my mom, the same one who had fallen out of my life, was worried about my situation. "Yeah, it's me, Mom. Slow down, though, and stop acting like everything is fine between us."

Mom: "Right. But can you tell me what happened and why you haven't given yourself in? I know I was a terrible person to you after your sister left, but I never thought that you would kill someone."

I wanted to hang up the phone at that moment. Hang up because my mom, the mom who hadn't spoken to me in years, was now blaming me like she always did. She was perfect; I was the violent one. I decided that if it was going to be most likely the last time I was going to talk to her for a couple of years, then I might as well speak the truth.

"Yeah, Mom. Look, I didn't kill anyone. I'm going to try to explain to you what's going on, and I don't expect you to believe a single word, but if you listen and don't judge it immediately, then we can talk about it."

As soon as she acknowledged my words with a quick "okay," I started from the beginning. Starting from all the times that she wasn't there. I talked about the essay I wrote to get into Harvard, and finally, I talked about my mental state during these sensations. "So I'm safe, I'm with my friend, and we are going to figure this out, trust me. All I ask is for you to stay off the news for a while until all this is resolved."

As I finished, the sound on the phone switched on and off with static for a while. I think, for the first time in my life, my mom was listening to the words I spoke. She didn't say anything for about three minutes; three minutes would normally be awkward, but at this moment, it was probably the most love I had ever felt from the woman.

Mom: "Wow, Jess. Uhm, I can't even describe the amount of pain you've been through. I forgot you were going to Harvard until your sister told me last year, but I didn't know it was because of an essay you wrote because of how terrible I was." As much of a disconnect was present between us, I think she still knew that the last thing I wanted to hear was an apology for the situations that had occurred between us three years prior. "Look, Jesse, I'm just proud of you and happy to hell that you're not actually a murderer, assuming you're telling me the truth. If I can help, I would get it if you don't want it, but I'm here for you and your friends."

I almost cried at that moment. I felt a tear roll down my eyelid, but at the moment, I was too stunned to know why. It wasn't just because of the actual honesty I felt from her, but also that I felt like she actually believed me. She had always hated the way I thought outside the box, looking at it as a waste of time. I had brought her an idea that was outside any box of reality, and she sounded willing to believe my perspective on it. "Thanks, Mom. I gotta go, but I love you."

I hung up before she could respond, mostly because I didn't think I was ready to hear her answer. Considering it was probably the first time I had said those words to someone in over three years, the last thing I wanted was for her to say anything except in agreement. The rest of that day, I didn't do much of anything. Even when Kira came back and tried to get me to help her with dinner or have a conversation about the day, I ignored her, quickly going to bed alone with my thoughts, thoughts that calmed my mind for the first time in a while.

When I look back on this night, I ask myself whether this whole situation was a gift or a curse. Was the pain and fearfulness of it, unlike anything I had experienced? Yeah, of course, but at the same time, the trauma had gained me a friend in Kira, a new understanding of how exceptional a "normal life" is, and most importantly, a progressing relationship with a woman that I thought could never be pieced back together.

The next day, I was woken up by a call from an unknown number on my phone. The moment I picked up, however, I knew it was someone I knew, that being Nicole. I simply said hi, which resulted in a five-minute rant by the girl about everything going wrong in her life.

Nicole: "So you're telling me my sister is putting our only father figure in a fire, and that the man who infected my uncle is still alive! Jesse, please tell me how this gets any worse."

From anyone else, these phrases would seem selfish considering the scenario, but not from her. "Look, Nicole, if I help explain everything about that and bring Kira for the uncle stuff, can you help me figure out what Jenkins told Kira and me?"

Nicole: "Yeah, of course, I would love to help you and especially to talk to my sister. However, I must make sure it's safe for you to be here. I will go ask. Just stay on the line, Jesse."

I waited on the phone, still only half awake, as the only sounds coming over the phone were the occasional siren echo from the hospital. "Okay, Jesse, you should be good. I talked to them, and they said as long as Kira comes with you and is screened, they won't alert anyone."

I nodded, saying "Okay" as I hung up. I got out of bed, got ready, and walked to the main room where Kira was. It was Halloween, a day that is normally known for the fantasies of ghosts and evil spirits. The only difference was that all of the elements that were a fantasy to everyone else were a reality for me. "Hey, Kira, we are supposed to go over to the hospital in a couple of hours, just so you know."

I don't know what I expected when I scheduled a meeting with her unstable sister without her knowing, but I was about to figure it out.

Kira: "Sorry, what did you do? You scheduled a freakin' meeting with my sister, who probably hates me to what, figure out whatever gibberish Jenkins told us is wrong. Yeah, good thinking, Jesse. Even if she says it's safe, remember where she is. I don't hate my sister by any means, but if you think this is the best course of action in this scenario, then I couldn't even begin to explain how incorrect you are."

I looked at her with a face of regret, only mustering out the meaningless words "I'm sorry" as I went to the kitchen to grab some type of breakfast.

Kira: "It's whatever now, but we are talking about exactly what you want to talk to her about, and if she gets off topic and starts talking about my uncle, then we are leaving. If you try to stay, I will leave and leave you with the rest of the insane people surrounding Nicole on every day."

I felt struck by each word that came out of her mouth. It was clear that I had knowingly struck a nerve, and while I regretted it, I just cared more about figuring out what was going on. In my mind, there would be time to apologize to her later, but for now, at this point, after dealing with this fear for almost a month, I didn't think I was being unselfish.

"Okay, well, I'm pretty much going to ask her about the thing Jenkins told us, going to ask him about what Will thinks, and about the whereabouts of Titan, and probably about how to prepare for a third, and possibly more, emotional trance."

She looked at me and smirked before turning back to her room. "Whatever you say, Jesse, just tell me when we need to go."

I nodded, looking into her eyes as I continued to eat the breakfast I made. Maybe Kira was right. Right that, Nicole would only make things worse and right that she just wanted me to confront Kira about their late uncle. As soon as I finished, I got on my phone to write out what I was going to ask her. About two questions in, however, I stopped, realizing there was no point in making the situation worse. I ended up scrapping the note and going back to bed for the next couple of hours before I alerted Kira to get in the car around one p.m. that day.

The drive to the asylum was surprisingly talkative. I talked through what I was going to say, trying my best to reassure Kira about the idea of going there. Somehow, at that moment, I had forgotten that Kira and her sister had gone through so much that she really didn't need me to make up some fake lie about how smooth the next hour was going to be.

About thirty minutes later, we got there, parked, and got out as we walked to the registration gate. Unlike the first time, the sirens and alarms that blazed on inside didn't faze me. I guess I had just come to terms with how weird of a situation this was, and I really wasn't going to let anything as seemingly simple as an alarm startle me. The lady at the front desk was told we were coming but still looked shaken.

Doctor: "Hi, uhm, are you allowed to be here? I know she's one of our resident's sisters, but you are under investigation, aren't you? I... uh, will be right back."

My heart dropped in that moment. I thought Kira had told me we would be fine. Did she lie? I was hopeful enough in Kira's sister that when Kira urged me to leave, I ignored her, standing pat as the lady walked around in the halls. I really wasn't too worried about authorities or anything. I was more concerned at that point about anything not going smoothly, at least the stuff that was supposed to. A couple of minutes later, she walked back, smiled, and led us into the back, where Nicole was without any dispute. I had no idea what she had just done, and honestly, I didn't want to. All I cared about was talking to Nicole and getting out of there as soon as possible.

Nicole: "Oh, hey, Jesse, Kira. Thanks for coming. I honestly thought you were going to blow me off because of my sister's worry about this conversation not going the way she thought."

I glanced at Kira before glaring back at Nicole. "Look, I get you're mad at her, and you're welcome to rage about that later. But I need to ask you about what I know, and I need you to give me an honest and non-emotional response."

Nicole: "Yeah, fine. But I am getting to Eli before you guys leave to go wherever you are even staying. I mean, honestly, though, Jesse, you should probably ditch her. I mean, you're in like federal trouble right now. It might not be good to be teamed up with a wildcard who will set fire to everyone you trust."

I ignored her. The thing I did know at that moment was that nothing good was going to come out of some type of severe disagreement between the two sisters. "Okay, so first off, when Jenkins was describing my case, he gave some weird transcript about a hearing interface or something that was infecting my brainwaves. I know it's not much, but he insisted that's all he could figure out."

Nicole: "Okay, Jesse, look. Before I try to help you and her figure out what he was even thinking, I want to ask you, how would you describe the emotions, the feeling across your body when these trances are occurring?"

It took me a second to process her question. As unconfusing as I wanted to be, any truthful answer wasn't going to make sense, so I figured I might as well just say the thoughts that came out of an emotional and scared mind. "I would say it's different than anything I've experienced in my life. I think the best way to describe it is to say it's unexplained. It's as if there was a void where time, space, and reality are suspended, and that's where my brain is taken. It's a takeover of my emotional state, most of the time resulting in speech deficits or phrases that I can't control. It feels like my emotions are in some sense of reality of endless possibility while the rest of my body lays in a realm of logic and emotion."

Nicole laughed slightly, not in the way of making fun but more an impression. "That's... wow, yeah, okay. As far as what Jenkins said, he may be right, and I don't know. A hearing interface sounds too specific for a man like him, but at the same time, it may be so different that even he doesn't really know what's going on. Anything else that could help?"

I nodded and thought as I stood next to Kira.

Kira: "Yeah, sis, Jenkins kept referring to his fear of Will's uncle Titan when it comes to these cases and was confident that whatever was causing this chose Jesse due to a quote, 'hurt emotion.'"

Nicole: "Okay, I didn't ask your opinion, but yeah, that makes more sense to this whole situation. If whoever is doing this really wanted to hurt you, you would be dead. It's obvious to me that whoever is doing this only wants to test your emotions or, honestly, to scare the living shit out of you. As far as the uncle, I mean, I know him. I also know he doesn't like cases like yours that are so unique, but at the same time, if you are taking advice from him, then I don't know why Kira and I are even here."

I looked at both as I debated whether to defend the man. I almost knew for sure that I would regret it if I did. But again, if Titan was really the genius and wrongfully convicted man that Will knew, then what was Jenkins not lying about? Assuming both Nicole and Will were telling the truth, Jenkins had put one person in custody, had one on the run for a crime he didn't commit, and had solved a total of zero impactful cases. "Look, I'm not going to defend the man that you think hurt your uncle, but according to Will, the man was a genius and actually solved your uncle's case before Jenkins convinced Eli to falsely convict him as the reason he was going to die. But going back to what you said…"

Kira stopped me at that moment before I could finish. "So, you think our uncle, a man of high intelligence, lied under oath when he knew he was going to die anyways? I really want to believe you, and I don't mind, Will, but I could never believe that." Nicole, on the other hand, said nothing, almost as if she was trying to believe the words that came out of my mouth.

"Anyways, if whoever is doing this wanted just to torture me, I really don't know who would do such a thing. The only person who ever hated me was my mom, who I talked to today and seemed very happy with our 20-minute conversation. So if someone is attacking me, then either I really did hurt someone in the past that I don't know about… or the pain and trances I'm experiencing weren't aimed at me and now are being deflected onto my train of thought." Kira and Nicole looked at me like I was blaming them. I tried to assure both of them I wasn't, but even if they weren't mad at me for doing so, they definitely had the idea flowing in their minds.

Our conversation went on for about another ten minutes before it started to migrate over to the autopsy and everything about the two girls' uncle. I had a feeling the conversation was going to drift into such, and I was just hoping for anything else.

Kira: "Look, Nicole, I did that, and it's not finalized, but it's being done to help his sanctity. I loved him just as much as you did, and his body being kept alive by some spell and the unburials isn't paying a type of respect to the man."

Nicole: "Fine, but that's not the fucking point, Kira. You never discussed it with me, you never thought to ask me, you didn't even tell me you were going to visit his body."

Kira: "It wasn't important, like honestly, the only good that was going to come out of it was the argument we are having anyways, like…"

JESSE OWENS, KIRA WHITTS, THIS IS THE POLICE. PLEASE COME OUTSIDE FOR QUESTIONING!!

At that moment, the conversation between the two sisters had turned from an argument to a truce to figure out how to get her and me out of this mess.

Nicole: "Okay, go out my window, around the back to the cellar. It will take you to the parking lot, and then it's all on you."

It wasn't the best idea, but it was truly the only shot we had. As Kira and I left the room, the sirens only got louder, the footsteps only heavier, until a knock on the door signaled the time to flee or give up.

As Kira jumped out the window with me following close behind, I didn't know if I would ever talk to Nicole again. As many differences as she and Kira had, she reminded me of my sister every time I spoke to her.

We proceeded to run across the back gate, crawling under the cellar and popping up at our car. Somehow, to my surprise, our car was not surrounded. As we jumped up, getting in and driving off at a speed that could only be described as reckless, I received a text from Will, more like a paragraph, but one of importance, stating...

Will: "My uncle responded. He said not to go near Jenkins and to meet him at 101 Blueside Rd over in Boston. I can't tell you whether to trust him or not, and honestly, his text seemed frantic, but if you need me to talk to him, I can since I'm the only one he is seemingly willing to communicate with at this moment. I would say he's trying to help, but again Amy doesn't even trust the guy, so if you and Kira don't want to, just tell me, and I'll let him know."

As I sat back in my seat reading the text, my mind and Kira's seemed to align with questions about the uncle. Why did Will know so much? Why did he trust the guy so much? Why was Will the only person he was consulting with, and finally, what was at the address that the seemingly innocent man disclosed?

CHAPTER 10
WILLIAM N. BLACK

As I wrote the text to Jesse, I honestly hoped that he was smart enough not to go to my uncle. The only reason I ever trusted him was due to our past; the way he helped me when I was most lost. But again, that didn't make him trustworthy. Amy and I sat back in her bed thinking the same thing: don't listen.

Amy and I had met about three years prior at school. It was one of those lucky situations where you can pull the girl of your dreams by purely walking the school hallways. She and I fit so well together that it was kind of astonishing. The only thing we disagreed on was my uncle, but even I had lost trust in him recently. It wasn't just because he wasn't responding to me, but more so because it counteracted everything that he had preached to me as a kid.

When I was growing up, my parents pretty much gave me everything I asked. Spoiled is a term they even used back then to describe a brat like myself. I would party, drink, get girls, and pretty much never focus on anything that was even directly important to the outcome of my life. The only reason I even went to college in Boston was because of my uncle, a man I first encountered when I was ten. It was 1987, and I had the one thing any kid would ask for: money to spend. I wasn't remotely smart with it, which led to disappointment on my parents' end.

When I first met Titan, I was honestly scared of him. He seemed like a very large human being, probably around 6'3", 240 pounds, and seemed more focused on his work than anyone I had known previously. At the time, he was simply a professor in Boston, but he always seemed to find a way to make time for me in my younger years. The one piece of advice he told me that I have never forgotten to this day was simple:

"Life doesn't get any easier, Will. You're incredibly lucky to have the parents you do, but if you're not willing to strive for what's unknown, then the known is all that will come to you."

The first couple of years after he told me that, I honestly ignored it. I felt like I was okay with what was already known because, like any teenager, all I wanted was a hot wife and kids. This idea of a perfect life pretty much eluded me, with every friend and girlfriend I had becoming more of a burden on life than anything else. The only two people I met who were any different were Jesse and Amy. I met Jesse junior year, and honestly, I made fun of him at first. Jesse was a loner, to say the least, in high school. The few times he would come to parties, he would win every single drinking contest, clean up, and leave. The only thought I ever had of the kid was that he was simply weird. He almost never spoke to me but always had the smartest idea when it came to class and always had the highest tolerance for pretty much anything illegal.

The day I first really talked to him was the week after my uncle moved across the country. It was one of the hardest weeks of my early life, knowing that I would almost never again see him as much as I used to. I was 17 at the time, and Jesse, who was also 17, was put in my group for a two-vs-two debate project. Like I said, I was in such emotional pain that I kind of knew that I wouldn't be able to do much work when it came to the project. Honestly, the first thing I ever told him was, "I know this is going to sound like I'm lying, but my uncle just moved across the country, someone who was as close to me as anyone, and I can't promise my work on this is going to be that good."

Jesse: "I totally get that, bro. My uncle is the one I'm closest with, too. I got most of the work; just help me out in a couple of areas, and then with the debate, I'm not particularly good at arguing."

At the time, I obviously didn't know that we would become such good friends, but I did immediately realize how much he reminded me of my uncle. I was shaking. I didn't think anyone was even remotely close to him, but as the project went on and we got to talking more, I started to see each piece of Titan fall into Jesse: the expertise, the imagination for the unknown, and countless other significant things that made me wonder. I would almost say that day turned around my whole life, looking back on it. Jesse and I would continue to work together the rest of the year, even on separate projects, and the more I got to know him, the more I forgot about my uncle, who would only respond to me once a week.

In the first few weeks after he left, I would send him a text every day, describing the events of my life in detail. Each time, I hoped he would respond. But his replies were always the same: a simple, *"Hope you had a good week."*

No acknowledgment of my words. No follow-up questions. Just the same empty phrase.

This trend repeated itself for about a year. Fifty-six texts. Fifty-six *"Hope you had a good week"* replies. Fifty-six moments of waiting, hoping he'd add an extra word or two.

My relationship with the man I trusted most had dwindled to nothing more than a text. One text, sent at 8:45 every Saturday, brief and impersonal.

It wasn't my fault—I knew that.

The day I turned 18, I gave up. I was about to leave for college, and the last thing I needed was the weight of a man who didn't seem to care about me hanging over my head.

I stopped texting him entirely.

That was, until a week before college, when I sent him one last text. This one wasn't about my day or my achievements. It was about a girl I had met through Amy. Her name was Kira Whitts.

He proceeded to leave the message "unread", just as I expected, until an hour later when I got called by the same number. I was stopped in my tracks at that moment. I was on my way to get food and hang out with Amy, and now I didn't know what my day would be if I picked up. As much as I now resented him, I picked up, hoping he was going to say sorry, but I never would have guessed how much more he said.

Titan: "Hey, Will, I just want to say sorry for my lack of involvement in your life. I've responded to your texts to make sure you know that I'm here, but I know that probably think I don't care or that I am avoiding you"

I got back in my car at that moment, putting my seat up in preparation for a conversation that I knew was going to be difficult. "Look, I loved you, I still do, but are you in trouble? Are you even a teacher? You just moved across the country and ghosted everyone? Like, I don't even know you anymore."

Titan: "I know, son, I mean Will, but I can't tell you the truth for your protection, and as far as your new friend, she needs to know to be careful."

I laughed at this, which seemed to confuse him. "So not only do you expect me to just be okay with your job being 'top secret,' but you call me after a year and immediately threaten my friend. Like if you're not going to be truthful with me and explain everything, and I mean everything, then why did you even call me?"

He paused for a couple of seconds, seeming to contemplate whether he was going to start talking. I knew him well enough to think he would, but again, I hadn't spoken to him for a year, so I really didn't know.

Titan: "Okay, I'm not a teacher, but you must keep everything I say quiet, even to your friends, even to your parents. I'm working with a couple of people who have cases of infected reality in an attempt to figure out the unknown."

A couple of months before that, I would have laughed him off the phone and been madder at him than ever at the lies he was spitting. But something in his words had caught my interest.

Titan: "The first case I solved, but the patient didn't really take the diagnoses well. So now I'm kind of on my own. The only reason I'm telling you this is because of your friends. If I'm correct, one of them had an uncle named Eli who is a patient of mine. It's difficult to explain, but basically, I'm trying to save him from the work of my old patient. You cannot tell Kira."

I sat there confused. It was almost like how I see Jesse now, except for the fact that I had the answers, and I was still confused. Uncle Titan and I continued to talk for about 30 minutes about his job, life, and everything else you could think of. The rest of it, surprisingly enough, wasn't nearly as confusing. Well, all except when I asked him who else knew about his work, and he responded, "Nobody, it's too dangerous. I regret even telling you, Will." At that moment, I hung up, got out of my car, and went to the store I was initially going to.

I couldn't tell you exactly why I continued to ghost him for the next couple of weeks. The only reason I have ever come up with is fear, but that part didn't even make sense when I thought about it. If I were scared, I would have never asked my uncle the questions I did. If I were terrified of his answer, I would have never talked with him extensively after it. The more I think about it, the more I think about what could have changed. I wondered if my uncle would have never done what he did with Eli to put himself in such a poor situation if I was simply there for him.

The next long text we shared was on October 12th this year. Jesse had just experienced the unexplained, and like Amy and everyone else, including him, we had no idea what exactly was going on. Amy and I had left that night around eleven pm, thirty minutes after Jesse collapsed and was taken to the ER. I trusted Kira enough to keep him company and, more importantly, to deal with any immediate repercussions that such senses would create.

That night, Amy and I discussed what had Now, Amy didn't really like him all that much, considering the one time she talked to him, he was deep in the middle of one of his inquiries, but she at least did acknowledge his expertise. I had forgotten about the man, considering we hadn't spoken in almost a year. I knew he was wanted, and knew he was on the run, so I simply decided to send a text saying, "Jesse unexplained faints." I was shocked when he texted back a few minutes later. His text was not short and was not close to the "have a good week" he used to send, but instead, it was a drawn-out paragraph that I knew Jesse would have to hear. On top of the explanation, he sent one more text, talking about his innocence, the uncareful pride of a detective named Colin Jenkins, and one final sentence that said, "I tried to save him from the brain toll these require, but Jenkins is too deep in his mind. Any explanation he gives will be from his unstable mind, not the intellectual one."

Even though it was probably the most confusing thing he had ever said, I almost understood it. It was simply a warning to Kira and me, a warning not to trust the guy when it came to Jesse's case. I didn't know at the time that Kira was attached to Jenkins, or I would have never let Jesse and Kira gain such a friendship, go to Jenkins, and get us into this whole mess..

My uncle had only sent the text that I was about to send Jesse because he heard about Jenkins' involvement. I didn't totally believe him, but it seemed like my uncle had such a strong sense that Jenkins was going to ruin Jesse's life that he begged me in the text to send Jesse what he wrote.

What was weird about it was that it didn't seem important to Uncle Titan that they went to the address, but just that they acknowledged what he said. I didn't know the address he had left and was more confused when I looked it up. It led to some port called Marianna's Marina on the Merrimack River across from Haverhill. Why would my uncle want Jesse to go to a port in the middle of the state?

I wrote the text out with my uncle's message and the address and sent it to Jesse, hoping he would ignore it. My hope was Kira, who would take a second, third, and fourth look at anything that my uncle wrote. Amy urged me not to send it. While I would almost always listen to her in these tricky situations, I knew this time I couldn't. I had to send that text. I had to follow my uncle's word on a topic about which he had so much experience and pain

My uncle and I's relationship remains subtle at best. Knowing I'm the only one in our greater family that he will talk to is definitely a scary thought. Despite that, I was always going to ask him for advice. I was always going to be there for him if he really needed it because, at the end of the day, he cared for me, was the only reason I knew Kira, and as much as I sometimes regret it, was the only reason I'm a part of this mess.

CHAPTER 11
A FINAL CONVERSATION

As Kira and I drove, trying to get back to the house on that abandoned ranch as fast as possible, I thought about the text. Kira quickly warned me about anything coming from Will's uncle and was very against everything having to do with him. And while I wanted to align with her more now than ever, I did want to ask Will and Jenkins about what he thought. Hence, Kira and I indirectly ignored his text and drove to Jenkins. We both agreed that this was the only course of action if we wanted to figure out everything that was going on. I didn't trust Jenkins, but I figured it wouldn't make a huge difference to just walk it by him.

From what Will had told me, Jenkins and Titan hadn't had a very smooth past, so Kira and I discussed our course of action as she drove. "We can't bring up who it was from, right?"

Kira: "Probably not, no. Considering the first words in the man's text were to ignore Jenkins, then my guess is that resentment is mutual, at the least. As long as we disguise the text as coming from someone that's not Titan, then we should end up okay."

I nodded. I always wondered how calm Kira seemed during these situations. Maybe she was just as nervous; maybe there was a raging demon stabbing at her heart; either way, she was excellent at hiding it. Every time we were about to do something that was innate, Kira was always driving, telling me what to do and being there to answer any of my questions. And while I still didn't know much about her, she provided a calming presence that I needed beyond rational doubt at that moment.

The drive to Jenkins' residence was calm. Considering Jenkins didn't know we were coming and that we were now running from the police, the need for him to help us solve the case was only getting greater. We parked in front of his house, a residence that looked even more bare than the cabin Kira and I were residing in. It almost switched on and off from a place of comfort to the place of curiosity that he designed it to be. The only reason I understood why he wanted to be so distant from reality was Will. When he used to talk to me about his uncle, before the ghosting started, he would always mention how secretive his uncle's job was in terms of the traces to reality. As described by Titan, it was "a job that pulled your mind farther from reality the closer the solution came." Before any of this happened, I honestly wanted to do what the detective was doing now, but obviously, that was before I saw the massive effect it had on people.

As we walked in, Jenkins greeted us and invited us in, and we got straight to the point in such conversation.

Jenkins: "If you guys are still coming here so quickly after you were just caught, it must be important, right? I've looked even more at your case, and I can't figure it out anymore. This is the first case in which I really don't know how I can help the person."

I looked at Kira before turning back to Jenkins sitting on that same couch. For the first time in our couple conversations, I was confident when talking to him, "My friend figured out another piece to this, and we need your opinion on it. Basically, he disclosed a location to meet him in order to speak on the matter, but considering I really don't trust anyone except maybe Kira, I thought it wouldn't be a bad thing for a second opinion."

I laid back on the couch, looking at him. For some reason, it looked like every word I said resonated with him, like he heard them before.

Jenkins: "Okay, what was the place to meet? I'm assuming this isn't your friend with the uncle, at least I'm hoping you would tell me if it was. The location could probably give you better clue than anything I will find in the next week. I would go for it."

"101 Blueside Road."

Jenkins immediately walked over to his computer, pulling up a map of the greater Massachusetts area as he looked up the address I had just given him. He seemed frazzled at first, almost like the address I specifically told him had resonated with him.

Jenkins: "It's in the middle of the water, well, kind of. It's off a port on the Merrimack River. The only thing there is a festival they are hosting starting tomorrow night, but I don't know why it would even be slightly significant otherwise."

The more I thought about it, the more sense it made. Obviously, I wasn't going to tell Jenkins that the message was from Titan, but it really did make sense. A person who was as wanted as him would like to meet in a crowded but private area. Somewhere, nobody would expect a man like him to be. At the time, I still thought Titan could help, even if he wasn't part of the reason I was experiencing such trauma. "So, should we go," I asked Jenkins. It seemed like he thought the idea of the message was mostly insignificant, but it still seemed to revoke the opinion of the renowned detective.

Jenkins: "That's up to you, Jesse. I will talk to your friend about why he wants to do it. Even if the idea of the festival seems innocent, the minute you cut off your awareness is the minute that the 3rd scare will happen. Just call me if you need anything. However, I normally attend the festival as my way of getting out of the house once a year, so if you have any difficulties, I will be there to support you if needed."

I nodded in a confused manner. If Titan and Jenkins knew each other so well, then why would Titan want to meet up in the one place that his worst enemy was?. Every time I thought about it, I thought more about how Jenkins could have been the culprit. I know he was the detective and everything, but he just knew too much. Although if he was, why would I be the one he was scaring? I had never seen the guy before the previous week, and I had never even heard of the name before Kira told me he was the best option for help.

The conversation with Jenkins didn't last long, and it didn't tell me much besides the festival that was going on. The only thing Kira and I seemed to agree on after this interaction was that we needed to talk to Will to get his opinion on the text before we fully trusted it. The walk out of the car was a surprisingly relaxing one. Looking back on it, I think it was because Kira and I somehow knew that it would be the last time we would be in the detective's cabin.

Decades later, I still wonder about Jenkins' past. I knew that he was trying to help us. I knew that his motivation for solving such cases was high, but besides the small bits I had heard from Titan through Will, I basically knew nothing about the guy. He was so secretive, so discrete in everything that he did. It was the reason he even crossed my mind as the person who was controlling my emotions. His mysterious nature was too hard to predict, too hard to trust, and too hard to rationally contemplate what he was thinking.

Kira and I got in her car and drove over to Will's. When I called him, he was extremely hesitant about being involved, but after about five minutes of slight convincing and a reveal of our mysterious mindset about the text, he was more willing than ever to meet with us. Amy stayed home during our meeting, mostly due to her fearful nature and Will's desire to protect her from whatever was going on.

About an hour later, we met with Will on the side of 76th Street in a suburb just outside Boston. He looked surprisingly happy to meet with us as we walked into a house. He said his parents used it when they could come visit him.

Will: "As good as it is to see both of you alive, I need to know what we are trying to figure out."

Kira: "We need to know why you sent the message. I get you used to trusting this guy, but the address is simply a port on the Merrimack River, and Jesse and I don't know what to think."

Will: "Yeah, look, I was praying that you guys came to me before you went. When I tried to get him to tell me why it was so important to meet, he never responded, leaving me unread like every freakin' time!"

I nodded solemnly. I knew the relationship between him and his uncle was rocky at best at this point, and just like him, I was confused as to why the man was even communicating with Will. Will had tried so hard to keep in touch when Titan had first left, and now, he was being told a bunch of stuff that could get him in trouble if ever revealed. "Why did you tell us then," I asked him, looking into his hurt eyes. "And do you think we should do what he said?"

Will: "Honestly, I don't know, Jesse. I told you because he claims to have been been right about the other cases, so if he is tracking yours, he can probably give you some type of clue that you obviously aren't getting from Jenkins. Considering I don't even trust the guy anymore, it would be hypocritical for me to suggest you go, but as long as you're careful about it and safe with at least Kira, then you should be okay."

I agreed uneasily to go, but also asked Will to come with us. I understood when he was hesitant, but after calling Amy, he decided to help us, considering his girlfriend was safe. So there it was: Will, Kira, and I were on a new journey, hoping to find out whatever this was so we could move on with our lives.

The first thing we had to figure out, however, was how I was going to get into the festival. Obviously, I couldn't just check in like a normal person, considering my name and face were all over the news. We had to figure out a way to sneak into the festival through the water, closer to where Titan had initially said we should meet. With any other people, this might have been impossible. But considering Will's family had a fleet of small speed boats, and Kira seemingly could always figure out solutions to anything at this point,, my confidence was well past zero.

About an hour later, the three of us hopped in Will's car and drove out of the neighborhood that Halloween night. The start of the festival was just about 24 hours ago, and we had a lot of work to do. As we drove to his parent's place on the water, glimpses of my younger life came across my eyes. I saw groups of kids laughing as they went from house to house in their costumes, families following close behind with a grin that could only mean half of their child's candy would be donated. Up until I was 16, that was life – a life filled with joy and excitement about the one day I would be able to stay up late and eat sugar out of my mind. It seemed like such a fantasy nowadays that the sight of joy made me weak in my knees. Besides a couple of laughs, the only pleasure I had experienced in the past month was for the few intervals once another step had been taken to reach the end. All I wanted at that moment was a sense of security, a sense of hope that all the work and preparation we were about to do for this festival wouldn't be a waste.

We parked outside the waterfront house about two hours later. The car ride was surprisingly quick as Kira and Will switched off driving. Usually, I would be the one to drive, but the last thing we wanted to do was crash due to an uncontrollable third event that I was supposed to come.. Will's parents weren't home, but they had left the keys to the boat we needed on the kitchen counter. Will make sure not to mention I was the one with him during the message, figuring even if they liked me, that they wouldn't be roped into what couldn't be much more unpredictable. The three of us decided that we would spend the night there to decompress before leaving for the carnival around the start of the next day.

We didn't want to be anywhere near the public too early. I needed to stay hidden, just like Will's uncle. While being on the FBI's Most Wanted list might demand more attention from law enforcement, a murder suspect who killed a professor at one of the most prestigious schools in the world wasn't far behind.

Most of the anger directed at me came from students and parents of the kids who attended Harvard. Classes had been canceled for the past week and were scheduled to remain so until I—or whoever they thought was the suspect—was caught and confessed.

I was the number-one story on every local network but for all the wrong reasons. I wasn't a renowned alum or someone who had done something spectacular. Instead, I was a relatively unknown student accused of committing murder.

The only people who believed in my innocence were the few involved in helping with my case. Anyone outside that circle seemed risky to trust. Even the few friends I had at Harvard had blocked me after I ghosted their initial texts.

Those texts mostly consisted of shallow inquiries, people claiming they wanted to know my side of the story. But I was smart enough to know that if I told them the truth, they'd only think I was guiltier than they already did.

Kira had advised me early on to cut off contact with anyone I didn't fully trust, and I followed her advice. The only time I broke that rule was to call my mother.

That night, the three of us—Kira, Will, and I—sat watching a battered TV, doing our best to avoid the news. The last thing we needed was more stress about the next day's plan, which was shaky at best.

As we scrolled through channels, we landed on Harry Potter. At first, the ticker at the bottom of the screen seemed like a usual weather update for the festival. But after a few seconds, my eyes began twitching rapidly.

Just like in Kira's car, my body and emotions felt normal and in check, but my eyes twitched differently. The message on the screen began to blur and shift, bold letters emerging:

"The festival of November is a fun and chaotic place of great measure, and as former Harvard alum Jesse Owens described, it is a haven of dream reality."

When my vision cleared, I realized Kira and Will had seen a completely different message. Neither of them noticed any change in my behavior or mood.

I knew this wasn't the third event I'd been anticipating, but it was a sign—a sign that tomorrow wouldn't be a waste.

I looked at Kira and Will, trying to figure out how to explain it. But before I could think of the right words, I blurted out:

"The festival is the end of this. And while it might kill me, it will solve the pain I'm living in."

CHAPTER 12
THE FESTIVAL

Will and Kira looked at me in distress and shock. It's not like I knew what had happened, but I had still seen it, unlike the two of them. When they asked about it, I tried to explain it, but I couldn't remember what the text had said. All I told them was that it would be resolved tomorrow, but I didn't know what would be resolved.. Was it why I had these trances? Was it how Kira's uncle had dies? Was it why Will's uncle was wanted by the police? None of us knew, all hoping for the same thing: an end to the chaos.

The next morning, I woke up excited but scared for what I would discover. Looking back on that morning, I realize it was probably the most nervous I had ever been. Nothing could prepare me for what was about to happen, what I was about to say.

The early part of the day was spent planning in a more precise way. All three of us knew it had to be perfect. From the entrance to the meeting to the avoidance of being seen, everything had to go right, though, none of us honestly thought that would happen. Something was going to get complicated. We just didn't know what or how different it would be. Kira and Will were both on calls during this time: Will was with Amy, and Kira was with her sister. The conversations consisted of a warning that nothing was going to be the same after that night. Ideally, we would have a conversation with Uncle Titan and find a solution But the idea of that seemed very unlikely. We really didn't know who we were meeting, considering it had been years since Will had seen him.

Around 5:30 p.m. on November 1st, 1996, we drove to Marianna's marina, hoping for a miracle. The plan was simple: Kira and Will would walk in as guests. They would then create a diversion using Will's speedboat malfunctioning, which would allow me to enter through a crowd of people without tickets. After that, we didn't know. The dock where Titan said to meet was unknown; he never told Will what boat he was near. I think we all just thought that if we got in, then we could figure the rest out from there.

About thirty minutes later, we were there. Will parked his car in the back lot, and just like we had planned, the rush hour of the festival was rising. Kira and Will got out, and I stayed in the car, waiting for them to text me once they got in. As Kira and Will got in line, I thought about what I was about to do. Nothing was technically illegal with the chaos we were about to create, but at that point, every risk felt like it was hard to execute. The amount of effort we were all putting in so that we maybe could get a piece of the puzzle from a wanted criminal seemed crazier than anything. If I had thought about that then, perhaps that night would have changed. But by that time, Kira and Will were already inside.

About fifteen minutes later, Kira texted me, simply saying, "Now," as I heard a loud crash over by the water. As I sprinted towards the entrance, trying to catch up with the greater group, the fear of what I was doing resided over me. If I got caught, I was alone, going to jail for murder with a chance of my life being over. Once I caught up, I put my hoodie on, looking down as I walked past the security and into the festival. The plan had worked: step 1, over.

As I made my way through the festival, it became apparent to me how similar it was to the first night back on October 12th. Besides the fact that I entered alone instead of with a group, almost everything was the same. There were coasters rolling loudly to my right, games surrounded by the laughter of families, and food as far as the eye could see. I wasn't trying to think of this, but I did. Every second I did, my heart got colder until I felt a cold burn around my chest that could only have been related to the feelings and remembrance of the very first voice. While I wasn't hearing the screams, the feeling I had felt that night resonated within me as I walked through the crowd. The only thing that got me out of it was when I saw Will arguing with a guard about the scar his boat had created.

Will: "How do you just have a pole in front of my boat? It's dark out, and you think that your festival allows my parent's boat to get scratched because of it. Unbelievable!"

The only thing that stopped Will's bickering was a side-eye from Kira telling him that I had made it in. At that moment, Will handed the guard a hundred-dollar bill and walked back towards me.

Will: "That was almost too easy," he said as he laughed between the three of us. "Are we good, though? Jesse?"

I nodded. There was no chance at that moment that I was going to start complaining about some PTSD I had with theme parks. It wasn't important enough; there wasn't nearly enough time for anything that wasn't part of our plan. The three of us walked towards the port, looking at each boat for any sign that would remind us of Titan. Will was the last one to see him, but even then, it had been three years. The only look I got during our walk was from a couple of guards, but I was quickly was relieved when thye didn't give me a second look. The one thing we didn't know, however, was that one of them called his boss about a sighting of myself around what was called the 31st pier, or the first landmark of boats.

As we walked, the multitude of boats surrounding us became impressive. The fact that Will could get the boat and park it near here was lucky. Will tried to text his uncle once or twice to alert him that we were there, but to much of Will's dismay, the messages were unread. I started to wonder more and more if we were just wasting our time. If Titan really wanted to meet, why wouldn't he tell us exactly where he was instead of hiding at such a popular festival?

We walked around for a couple more minutes before I noticed Kira stop. She was staring at a tall man, probably around 6'2, and wearing a top hat with a hoodie. "Kira, who's that? Are you okay?"

Kira: "Jenkins."

Her words struck me with a knife. I know he told us that he was coming, but why was he over near the ports as opposed to near the concerts? Did he know where Titan was? Was he somehow the one who texted Will? We walked over to him together, making sure we were ensuring his identity before revealing ours.

Kira: "Uhm Colin? What are you doing here?"

Jenkins turned to us with a mysterious smile in his eyes. He seemed almost to be happy to see us but seemingly surprised that we were there.

Jenkins: "Hey, I mean, I did tell you and Jesse that I come every year. I see you brought your friend, Will…"

Will glared at him. They obviously knew each other besides just a mention between Jenkins and his uncle. No, the two of them had a history.

Will: "Yea, hey Colin, look, I don't really have time for your BS. I need to know why you're here. And don't get me with the stupid annual tradition bullshit because the party is over there, not over here."

Jenkins: "See, I guess it was a good idea to listen to him. He's the only sensible one out of you three. But yea, I heard the line Jesse told me about the address, so I'm simply here to solve this mystery while you kids have fun."

I looked at him with pure hate. I had heard about countless people being angry with the detective, and now that person was me. "If I really trusted you to make a single step of progress, do you think I would be here? If you were actually a truthful guy in how much you knew, would your only clue be something I told you? So please don't tell me to go fuck around on some games when the more work here is being done by us, not you."

Kira and Will looked at me with surprise, but they stood behind me in my words. I think they were more surprised than anything else. I was never a social kid, as I'd said, so the fact that I had just rattled off insults to the man who claimed he was helping, came as a shock even to me.

Jenkins cackled at my words as he looked around. "Please remember," he said as he looked around, winking at a multitude of security, "You're still a wanted man, Jesse Owens, and your only path to finding forgiveness just died with me."

As his words came to a halt, I was surrounded by multiple lights as a couple of men dressed in full black walked toward us. At that moment, I swear Kira came up with 100 things we could do, but the one thing we all knew we weren't going to do was give up. As

Jenkins walked off, we ran in the other direction, hearing the screams of the authorities as we jumped around into the crowd of the party.

The most known festival of the year had now become the center of a chase scene, with hundreds of people not knowing what to do. A couple of civilians joined the chase for us in the hope of gaining a form of respect, not knowing these guards didn't even have the authority to process me. The three of us ran around a corner, taking a small breath once we were behind one of the games and then running again down to the pier.

I don't think we had any sort of plan in this scenario. A part of me wanted to get back in Will's car and drive to Kira's ranch – the one place in the world where I had felt safe. On the other hand, we still had an uncle to find and a mystery to solve, so we continued to run, eventually finding a hole in the under-deck of one of the richest-looking yachts in the said marina.

I never figured out how they never saw us get on the boat, but after a half-hour, the shouting had been reduced to a murmur, and the flashlights that had previously glared at us were now dimmed. The place we sat was dark and showed only a tiny glimpse of the outside world due to a rip in the cloth that was plated to the window. Whoever's boat it was wanted they wanted it to be kept as secretive as possible They also wanted to have a place to escape reality.

Escaping reality – that was the name of the boat: a haven for the reality of dreams. A haven, I thought, was a safe space reserved for all thoughts that weren't allowed in the rational world. It was like my dorm, a spot for the spontaneous thoughts of a human to rest and develop until they wanted to be known. But again, why did the name of the boat matter? Even if it was another clue, the unpredictability of this entire event was so random that it was impossible to know we were going to be on the exact boat and the exact time that we were.

It was now 7 p.m. The festival had ended early, much to the dismay of all the "normal" people who had bought a ticket. Once we concluded that it was safe to at least get off the boat, Kira jumped out, walking off the boat and onto the pier in front. Will followed close behind with myself, but as we got to the overlook, a question reigned in all our heads.

Kira: "So I get it. We all might be phased from that, and we are lucky that we aren't all in prison, but we still have to find this guy and are no closer to doing so."

Will looked at her with distress. "I don't trust the guy, Kira. And as much as Jesse needs to get his clue and closure from this whole situation, I can't even promise you that the next hour we spend running and looking for my uncle won't be a waste."

I stopped for a second as I looked at both of them. As much as I trusted them, as much as I was going to listen to them, I was going to be the one to decide what the course of action was. "We must keep trying, Will. I'm the one who is wanted, not you guys, so if you want to go home, that's fine, but I'm staying."

Will nodded, and as I leaned up from the rail, a strong force from inside shattered me, sending me into a blackout, one that resulted in the third trance that I had been worried about for weeks. This one wasn't like the others. My body stayed still as my eyes projected fear into what I saw. The screeches, the pain, the fear were there more than ever. It flashed a picture of a boat, almost like it was a picture of the future. I saw Kira and I walking down to the dock where the boat lay: dock 45t. As I stepped onto the boat, I followed the sounds of terror down to the bottom floor, which revealed a hatch, a hatch that led to what seemed like a deep dark room. A room where laid a group of entrapped humans, ones that all looked like my dad, the same dad who had shown up once a year until I was ten, leaving something different every time..

The more I thought about it, the more sense the words Titan and Jenkins had made. Not only were the trances personal with the showing of my dad and the event at my college, but each time, I felt darkness was aligned with one of the gifts my dad would bring. The first time, it was a carnival toy; the second, a customized journal. And the third, a singular blocked man. I had finally figured out why I was chosen, and the only thing I wondered at that moment was whether my dad was the one injecting such sounds, such fears, the same ones I had each time he would enter the house.

CHAPTER 13
THE VOICE OF A CHILD

In what felt like a couple of minutes later, Kira shook me awake. I looked at her in shock as she and Will quickly knew that the third trance had been done.

Kira: "Thank God you're awake. What did you see? Do you know what to do?"

I nodded. A small part of me would have usually found a way to be angry at Kira for her seeming uncared for my well-being besides a simple phrase about how she was happy I was alive. "Yea I know where the sounds are coming from." My voice dropped into a solemn cry as I finished the sentence. I was hoping that whatever I was going to see was different from my dream. The vision of my dad, of children, was one that I couldn't bear.

I got up, turning my walk into a jog as I raced towards dock 45. I didn't know how accurate my dream was, and again, Titan still needed to be found, but at that moment, the only thing I cared about was figuring out what the sounds were. As we got to the dock, the first part of the vision came true:: a white, 2-layered boat floated behind the one flickering spotlight that still remained from the festival.

Kira, Will, and I jumped on the boat; none of us were ready for anything at that point. As I walked down the steps following what I remembered, a coldness surrounded us. This time, however, the coldness wasn't just for me but for the surrounding air that enclosed us. The only sounds were the thuds of our feet and the crashing of something below us, something that would align with the dreams I had just experienced.

To the right, a hatch lay against the back corner of the room. The only other thing in the room was a rope. I instructed Kira to grab it in case of emergency. The closer we got to the hatch, the louder the thumps got. Boom. Boom. Boom. Scrapes against steel, thuds that sounded to come from a group of people, a group of people trapped like the ones I had just seen.

As I stood back and waited as Will opened the hatch, flashes from my past appeared to circle back to me: this whole journey with Will, Kira Nicole and Jenkins, the relationship with my mother, and, my dad, a man I had resented since he had left. The emotions felt more alive than ever. As the latch opened, my worst fear became more and more clear. As the three of us looked down the black abyss, the only thing that was there was a group of about six children, children around seven years old, children who were trapped, and children whose voices echoed against the crate were reminiscent of the original voices I had heard on October 12th.

Kira: "Holy shit, guys, where's the rope?"

The next twenty minutes were spent by the three of us working together to help each child out of the bottom, so they could reach a breath of fresh air. After each child climbed out, they didn't say anything and proceeded to run out of the boat, out to a world where they had no home.

As Kira and Will closed the hatch, the three of us sat in that enclosed room without anything to say. None of us knew how such sounds were transmitted, how they even got into my mind, and finally, where the children had come from?

The more I thought about it, the weirder it got. Seven children wasn't a coincidence. The location wasn't a coincidence. Nothing was.

Kira: "Look, do we even need to ask why or how? Like Jesse, you said you knew why it was you. What did you mean by that?"

I coughed, looking up at her. No word I said that night carried any confidence, yet they still came out.

"I never said I knew why I was chosen. I just said this whole thing hasn't been a coincidence. Seven wasn't just a random number of kids—it was the number of years my dad came around, once a year.

"Three trances weren't random either. It was the number of gifts he brought each time, somehow hoping it would be enough.

"And forty-five… forty-five wasn't just a random dock. Forty-five was the number of hours my dad was alive after my uncle killed himself."

Kira looked at me with shock. I wasn't surprised. It was the first time I had ever disclosed my past, the reason I was always so quiet and the reason I could always drink the most. My dad was never in my life; he was in and out every April 11th for seven years until until an argument would occur between my mom and him.

Will: "Shit, bro, I didn't know. So, who do you think did this…"

I sighed as I looked at him. "Jenkins wouldn't have solved this because it was impossible to do so unless he was me. It almost seems like it was more of an attack on him than me." I wasn't going to explain it to Kira and Will at that time because I could barely comprehend how personal the whole thing was when I thought about it in a greater picture.

It all started when I was four. The first time I remember seeing my dad, the first time he gave me a gift. and the first time, I never thought he was going to leave that time. The screams weren't random. They weren't meant to be from the kids trying to escape. They were the echoes of the exact words I would say in my mind every time he and my mom fought. Each time my dad would come over, he and my mom would fight for about twenty minutes. He would kiss my sister, leave three toys for us, and then walk out, not to be seen again for another year.

By the time I was seven, I started to wish he wouldn't come back the next year. He only caused pain when he would come, and no matter what he thought, his quotes about "how much he loved and cared about me" never really meant anything after the first time. I had come to terms early in my life with the fact that having a dad just wasn't in the picture. And as much as I also tried to cling to my uncles, it never was the same. It was the reason I stayed alone so often; I was used to it. My essay for college wasn't just about my mom's struggles with being there but also the forgiveness that I gained for her the more I thought about how bad my father was.

Kira: "So do you think your dad is the one punishing you for not loving him back as much as he thought he deserved."

I shook my head, explaining that he had died, but again, her words resonated with me. My dad was so focused on what he thought was being a good father that he never asked me or my sister. According to Emma, he was there for her before I was born but started to argue more and more with my mom after she got pregnant.

The idea that I was the reason my dad hated everyone so much was a tough one to deal with. From a young age, I dealt with the burden of being the only guy in a house of pure chaos. Like I've said, my mom tried her best, but her best just was never good enough. The screams I had were not just the exact ones I had rattled off but in the order of the ones that hurt the most. As much as I wanted to keep it in, I decided to explain to Will and Kira about the whole situation that had happened over the past month.

"The original shrieks I heard were from a young child, that young child being me at four years old. It was the first time that I actually thought that he was going to come back. For some reason, a part of me would cry out the same words, asking where he was and why he seemed to hate me. I have no idea how the man died, but when I was ten, and he left for what I didn't know was the last time, I cursed him out in the journal I was writing., 'Screams of death, dead or alive, the echo's are real,' were the first three lines that started my journal back in 1987. I didn't even know the man or anything he did when he left. My mom would always make up some story about how he was doing secret undercover work that couldn't be disclosed, but that lie stopped as soon as she knew my sister and I were smart enough to comprehend."

Our conversation lasted a little longer, mostly with more explanations of my rocky past more than anything else. Kira and Will sat silently across from me as I spoke but didn't say much as I poured out my life to them. "My entire life has been a lie, guys. The only thing that hasn't been a lie, is all of us in the past month. It's why I have let it take over my life."

Will: "Yea, bro, look, we are here for you, me, Kira, Amy, all of us. No matter what Jenkins, my uncle, or your dad thinks, you're a genius and the only person who I honestly think would still have the motivation to solve it. You know, when you were passed out that first night, the reason I told Kira that it wasn't anything like something supernatural was that nobody I know besides you would be willing to fight it."

Kira, however, who was always focused on the last steps we still had to solve, cut the end of Will's speech off though, stating, "Look, I would love to give you love, but we still haven't found his uncle or whoever is creating this."

As I nodded and looked up, I quickly realized a shadow had appeared on the upper deck, and no, I wasn't just seeing it this time. As the three of us walked up and saw the figure in the shadow, we were shocked. The 6'5 man stood in front of us and simply said, "Found me."

CHAPTER 14
AN INDIRECT NIGHTMARE

We had just spent the last hours trying to find Will's uncle, when he had been was on the boat with the children the entire time.

Titan: "Good to see you guys; I'm glad you made it in one piece." It was almost like the whole situation was a joke to him. If he was the one who had infected me, then why was he acting like nothing had happened? Why was he acting like his entire plan had just worked?

I looked for any reaction from Will or Kira before I spoke up. "Yea, hi. What did you want from us? Because after what I just saw, I really don't have time for games."

Titan: "Of course, sorry. Follow me."

We followed Titan off the boat and onto the pier below. There wasn't anyone else around. We thought that Jenkins had left, so we thought we were all alone. I really couldn't tell you why we were so willing to trust uncle Titan besides desperation, but what else were we going to do? We walked for only a couple of minutes before we got on another boat as Titan stopped on the upper deck.

Will: "OK, so get to your point. I feel like I'm being left 'unread', for God's sake. Like seriously, the three of us have been trying to help Jesse for weeks, and all you have said were some clues that, while got us to the source, have made this situation weirder."

Titan: "Look, nephew, did you ever ask yourself how I knew so much? Why could I tell you exactly where to go?"

The three of us looked at each other in disbelief. Was it that obvious? Was Titan the one who was controlling this? But again, why would he do this to me? I didn't even know the guy, much less understand how he could even do what he did. "You're saying you're the one who did this to me?" I wasn't even mad, just confused. I never did anything to anyone in my life except my mom, but besides that, I pretty much did nothing my whole life until I met Will.

Titan: "Yes, it was me, and I'm sorry Jesse. But if it makes it any better, it wasn't directed at you," he said as he sighed before disclosing the actual goal. "It was meant for Kira, the girl who helped Colin put me under investigation."

Kira: "What? I was helping Jenkins a bit, but I never advocated for him to put any of you in jail, including my literal sister. Plus, how did you mess up so badly and direct it at Jesse. He did nothing to you."

Titan sat back against the pole on the pier and started to explain how the process works. After weeks of trying to figure out the who and how, assuming he wasn't lying, it was all being revealed. As he spoke, I really didn't know what to think. My first thought was to be relieved, but again, this conclusion really wasn't going to get me out of prison, really wasn't going to get Jenkins off the case.

Titan: "It's complicated, Kira. In my 10 years of actually helping suspects prior to it, I had figured out that infecting a single brainwave with an idea from their past would spark a viral scent of emotions for weeks until they figured out how to control them. Your friend did a surprisingly good job for the amount of reminiscence the device put into his past."

Titan leaned back, grabbed something from the boat cabinet, and handed it to me. It was a simple transmitter that looked more like a current-day camera, but for the late 1990s, it was a piece of art. As the three of us looked at it, I was confused. "So, if Kira had been the one infected, would there have been those kids, or would it have been something else? How personal really is this device?"

Titan: "I won't get into what Kira's past, but it was designed to affect the specific person it targets. For Kira, I don't know what it would have done, but for you, it was obvious. The device is also the reason Kira's uncle is still alive. I didn't kill him. I simply did it after he was dead, but even saying that pretty much traces a path through what you are most sensitive about."

Will: "Then how did Kira's uncle die anyway? That's another thing you refused to tell me. And if it was really you that caused this, why would you give us clues."

Titan: "As far as Kira's uncle, he died with a severe case of brain cancer he attracted while Jenkins was running tests. So no, Jenkins didn't directly kill him or even know how he died, but the original lacerations that you saw on his brain were from the surgery, not the undead nerve that was popping. As far as why, it was simply because I wanted to help you guys solve Jesse's problem before Jenkins could."

I looked at him in pure confusion. How did he even know that Jenkins was involved? And I know there was a weak spot in their relationship, but I never thought that it would result in the trauma that I had been through.

Titan: "I was mad at myself after I convinced Jenkins to join this line of work after he dealt with it himself. I was trying to create a case he couldn't solve using someone I knew he cared about in Kira. I really didn't mean to ghost you, Will, or to put you through this, Jesse, but it's been clear to me that you are the only one who could have dealt with it."

As much as he was seemingly trying to be friendly, I wasn't buying it. A guy who had caused so much pain was now trying to act like he didn't do anything on purpose. "So, you thought if Jenkins failed to solve mine, he would quit, leave the life that you two somehow enjoy?"

Titan: "Yes. I thought if Jenkins was truly so far from solving it or a case that seemingly had zero clues besides the ones I was sending you."

Will, Kira, and I really didn't have words for the guy. I was almost happy at that moment that I was the one who was infected. I don't think Titan even realized that even though it was painful, it was the best journey I had ever been on in my life. My life had been a stream of lies, starting with a dad who didn't want another kid and finishing a college acceptance because of the hate I had for my mother. Now, I was never going to give Titan such satisfaction, but as I stood there confused as ever, such thoughts did pass my mind.

As we continued to talk, I started hearing a thud that seemed to come from another person on the boat. "Do you guys hear that?"

They nodded, and as we looked back, the man in the hat was there again; Colin Jenkins was still on the pier, watching the whole time.

Kira: "Colin, what are you doing here?" She glared at Titan before looking back at Jenkins, almost in the mindset that they were working together.

Jenkins: "I simply heard a couple of lies that I couldn't wait to inject on. It's interesting, however, about how your uncle, Will, went after your best friend instead of little old me, who he knew would laugh at any sensation that I would've received. Funny what anger and jealousy do to a person."

Will looked at his uncle with disgust. "So, I need the truth right now, Uncle Titan. I don't even know why I'm still acknowledging you as a part of my family, but either way, the truth, now."

Titan: "When I first came to Jenkin's case, I tried to work with it while in Boston, but I never could find the peace in my life to do it. So your aunt and I moved to LA, which did help in that case; but I do regret it. After I was in LA, I decided to help with cases out there for the next couple of years. I was responding normally then to try to keep our relationship, but after I moved back to Boston when Colin called me, I knew it was better to put our relationship on pause."

Will: "Fine, but look, why is Jenkins here? If you didn't want him to have any clue, obviously, the guy is smart enough to figure this out without any of your helpful clues."

Titan: "Wrong, Will. The only reason he's out here is because Kira had him roped in from the beginning. Everything with Jenkins has been a lie; the blaming of me for the person he killed, the insane want to continue to experience the rush of these scenarios even when he knew the pain it caused."

I was stunned. I really had nothing to say. Part of my speechlessness was because I didn't ever think I would get such closure about everything that had happened. All of it made sense now: the Kira and Will conversation at the motel, the calmness of both that first night at the park, the willingness of Kira and Nicole to debate over the sanctity of Jenkins, all of it just added up. Jenkins and Titan had indirectly destroyed countless lives that seemingly got in the way of whatever battle they were trying to have between them.

Jenkins: "Oh, the lies, it's actually insane. You know, if you ever just listened to me in the first place, none of this would've happened."

The next moments would replay in my mind for years after. Jenkins would pull out a pistol, shooting Titan in the chest three times as he pushed the bloody body into the Marianna's River. Will stood shocked as anger built up in him. The next moments moved at half speed as we stood in front of him to prevent anything from escalating. Jenkins would run off into the night, and the three of us would fall to the ground around the blood of the man who had caused the pain.

I didn't know what to think. None of us did. Will seemed obviously hurt to his core about the death of the man who taught him how to be a man. Kira seemed shocked that a person she thought she knew had just murdered someone in cold blood over a simple dispute. And me, who sat there wondering if I should be relieved or scared that the man who had created my misery was now lying under the ripples of the river.

The thing was, however, that it wasn't just some small dispute. It was a lifetime of agony for two men who were way too used to the pain of their experiences. Both men had come so close to the end of countless mysteries that it almost seemed like they had shared a moment of pride as this case had been solved.

I was so caught up in the moment that I didn't realize the sirens that continued to get louder. The closer they came, the more my brain seemingly fought the urge to hear them. I was tired of running, tired of being a nobody, tired of just being some kid in my dorm who would think about what was possible. I now knew the limitations of the amount of pain the worst people could affect on me . Will and Kira had left, and I was sitting there on the boat's steps, alone but unafraid.

Nothing a court would say would have phased me at that point. The worst thing was a case of murder built on no evidence that would be tried and would add some bogus thing to my resume. I no longer cared about school, or my studies. The only thing I cared about was revenge on Jenkins, and I hoped that I would be the last one ever to experience such misery. It was the most challenging month of my life emotionally, but somehow, I felt a certain peace.

It's why I was okay with Kira and Will running when the sounds of the sirens were approaching. As I looked to my right, I saw Titan's body floating in the red-painted water below. It was the end of a platform, a platform of rocky temptation and misery that was going to end with me in the back of a cop car.

I didn't know my future at the time or if I would even see Kira or Will ever again, but I was going to be at peace with whatever was decided. As I stood up and walked over to the sirens I had fled from, I, for the first time in my life, felt a sense of closure that I was questioning just minutes before—the end of the trances, the end of the mystery, the end of the questions.

CHAPTER 15
BACK TO NORMAL?

"So, what happened, how did you end up here?" Nicole said, looking across the table at me.

"Well," I began, "the court found a trace of my fingerprint on the wound that seemed to kill the teacher, and I was about to go to jail until testimony by Will, and Kira convinced the judge to move me here, with you."

Nicole and I became pretty good friends. Two people trapped in an asylum, convicted or things we didn't commit.

As for Kira, she and I talked about once a month during my time here. She became a mother, married to a guy I had met and introduced to her between the court appearances back in 1996. Kira knew she was wrong for running and continued to apologize for months after. I told her I was never going to leave that night no matter what she and Will had said. I needed closure, not another run. I was honestly more satisfied with the life I was currently living as opposed to one of "freedom" in an outside world that wanted me dead.

To this day, I have never really figured out Detective Colin Jenkins. Until Titan, he never struck me as an evil man. I trusted him that first Friday night in 1996, but he never again would have that same trust. There were just too many things about him that weren't normal. He was unlike Sherlock Holmes or any other detective you will read about. Instead, Jenkins was a man who seemed serious but also a joker who seemed to succeed only due to his unwillingness to be scared or have any fear. He had gotten away with Titan's murder, as the body was found five years later off the coast in a different state. The body was too spoiled for any inquiry to be done. The three of us decided it was pointless to try and find him at that moment. Jenkins had gotten away with murder and seemingly disappeared.

Will ended up marrying Amy. He would be cleared of any wrongdoing involving my case about a year after. He and Amy had a kid during this time, naming him after his late uncle, who was always there for him when he was just a boy. Will visited a lot less than Kira, mainly because his job prevented him from being anywhere near Boston. Every time he was in town, he'd swing by for a quick conversation. The conversations were not about us, but about how to keep his kid out of a world that we knew too much about. He even sometimes murmured at helping me escape. Like I said earlier, though, I didn't really have a reason to escape.. The people around me knew I wasn't insane. They saw how well I could communicate and think, which is probably why I got more freedom than anyone else in there, including Nicole.

Nicole and I's conversations were the most normal ones I would have while I was there. We would normally discuss what we were planning on doing once we got out. We even brought up the idea of getting married, which was crazy, but again, we were stuck in an asylum, so was anything really that insane?

The one topic I remember was a conversation we would have around 11 p.m. one night. When it was about more deep topics, Nicole and I would generally figure out a time to sneak out of our rooms once everyone had gone to bed so that we had some privacy. It was December 12th, 2001, and Eli Whitts was once again the topic.

Nicole: "Did Kira ever give you any explanation as to why she was cremating him?"

I shook my head. "No, but considering she was right about it being the best way to honor him and knowing this type of dark magic, with his afterlife being contained and infected with whatever that nerve is still doing, then I really don't know what to say, Nicole. I mean..."

Nicole: "I get that you agree, Jesse, but did she say anything about why she did it?"

I sat back and thought about each word that Nicole said. "Yeah, I mean, when she did it at first, I was confused when she didn't really ask you about it. She just said that it was the right thing to do, basically the same thing she told you when we came here for the last time."

As I thought more and more about the past decade, I still really can't figure out the whole situation. I really had felt a strong sense of closure back on November 1st, but I didn't even know what all my stress was for. I mean, Jenkins was the real question, and he was still free. Kira and Will were living their everyday lives as if nothing happened, but the pain of that month still managed to overcome them, as far as they told me. Maybe they were just doing this to keep me from actually going insane due to the constant number of dreams I would have about the past, as I constantly hoped I wasn't the only one.

Those were all they were, though: dreams. The port and marina were exactly what that text had said: a port of the wildest dreams to sleep. I would never end up going back to that port with a fear that the secretiveness of the place wasn't just going to stop at Titan.

Speaking of Titan, I had learned more about him through conversations with Will early on in my residence. Titan was a smart kid as a boy. He did go to college but didn't use his major. Instead, he spent his middle life on a boat, working for little money as a sailor. He lived on the boat, only getting money from the occasional tour or fish he would sell, but besides that, the boat was everything to him.

Titan, or whatever his full name was, had gone from an innocent sailor to a magic controller, one who had accidentally inherited a terrorizing power beyond his control that was sure to attack another innocent teenager again when they least expected it. Titan was dead, but the device was supposedly hidden by Kira as soon as she heard the sirens. She had told me that she had put it in hiding across the ocean somewhere at some house in Europe, but even that seemed like a stretched-out lie.

Nicole: "I just don't understand why she wouldn't include me in that decision. I mean, it's a man who helped raise both of us, and now she what? She thinks my opinion doesn't matter anymore?"

As much closure as I had gotten from that last night, any closure Nicole had about her uncle was now gone. She was pissed at her sister, and seemed like she wanted revenge.

"You can't do anything about it, Nicole. Your uncle is dead, and his remains have been reduced to dust."

Nicole: "You forget I get out in a month, Jess. My sister, who has lived her life like she has been such the perfect person, has now gotten you in here, and my uncle dusted off. I hope she is careful with what she decides to get herself into next."

I was still friends with Kira, and she was someone I cared about a lot. Now, the worry of her sister going after her was in front of me. The only way I could warn her was to wait until the next time she came and then let her know.

That next time wouldn't be until a week before Nicole was going to be out. She hadn't directly brought up revenge again, but at the same time, she didn't seem any happier whenever I brought her name up. The time was short, but my message to her was clear:

"I know I can't do much here, but Nicole's coming. She gets out in a week, and her anger is fully directed at you. I don't know how, but she is as unstable as ever and angry, and as she said":

Watch Your Back!"

*****

www.ingramcontent.com/pod-product-compliance
Lightning Source LLC
Chambersburg PA
CBHW040823010826
48978CB00012BB/593